The Scheme

Alexis V

Copyright@2017 Alexis V.

The moral right of the author has been asserted. All characters in this publication are fictitious and any resemblance to real persons, living or dead is purely coincidental. It bears no legitimacy to the actual world or any person or organization in it. Cover design by Peter Vincent.

All rights reserved.

No part of this publication maybe reproduced, stored in a retrieval system or transmitted, in any form or by any means, without the prior permission in writing of the author, nor to be otherwise circulated in any form of binding or cover other than that in which it is published and without a similar condition including this condition being imposed on the subsequent purchaser.

ISBN-13: 978-1548147051

Dedication

In Memory of Muriel
Mother and Encourager

Acknowledgements

I wish to thank everyone who support my writing ventures and in particular my friend, Leigh Turner Ph.D. who once more gave of her time and provided inspiration and encouragement as I was writing this book.

As always and in particular, forever gratitude goes to my husband Peter. He has enabled my aspiration of writing merely for personal enjoyment, to expand into an activity of significant writing development. Peter's wholehearted support for my writing pursuits continues to be profound. His design help is priceless and I thank him for the work which he continues to do on the cover designs of all my books. Last in order of mention but not of importance, is thanks to God, who enables my imagination and enthusiasm for writing.

Contents

The Scheme ... 1
Copyright@2017 Alexis V. ... 2
Dedication ... 3
Acknowledgements ... 4
Chapter One ... 8
Chapter Two ... 14
Chapter Three ... 25
Chapter Four ... 32
Chapter Five ... 40
Chapter Six ... 50
Chapter Seven ... 64
Chapter Eight ... 82
Chapter Nine ... 86
Chapter Ten ... 97
Chapter Eleven ... 103
Chapter Twelve ... 113
Chapter Thirteen ... 120
Chapter Fourteen ... 124
Chapter Fifteen ... 137
Chapter Sixteen ... 150
Chapter Seventeen ... 158
Chapter Eighteen ... 170
Chapter Nineteen ... 180
Chapter Twenty ... 185
Chapter Twenty-One ... 193

Chapter Twenty-Two 200

Chapter Twenty-Three 208

Chapter Twenty-Four 214

Chapter Twenty-Five 229

Chapter Twenty-Six 236

Chapter Twenty-Seven 247

Chapter Twenty-Eight 254

Chapter Twenty-Nine 265

Chapter Thirty 269

Chapter Thirty-One 279

Other Books by This Author 281

Books 282

Chapter One

It was Friday and the evening's sun had long disappeared behind the clouds. Within the walls of a London back street city office, all keyboards fell silent apart from one; Sage just had to put in more over time to earn extra money. She worked as a review writer and blogger for a small advertising company.

Sage now resentfully thought that she could have done this work at home, but the manager Jian demanded that all work had to be carried out on the business premises.

Everyone knew that Jian was always guarded and inclined to conceal intentions both personal and professional. He was not one to disclose any information apart from what was absolutely necessary so no work could leave his company. Sage sensed that Jian trusted no one and seemed to be very solitary.

To end her week's work Sage simply wanted to complete four more blogs to be paid enough to settle some of her mounting commitments. In Sage's mind, these bills had rapidly grown from ant hills to Himalayas. She could attribute her dire predicament to Parker her boyfriend who did have a habit to maintain.

Arguably though, she guessed that Parker was right. It was really her failure to budget properly along with her overindulgence in spoiling her two children that had caused this mess; Parker had repeatedly said. Sage mulled over these thoughts as her coworkers started their weekend exodus from the office.

"See ya later Sage." Kendal said. He was one of her colleagues and a very good friend. He was tall, handsome, dark skinned and trustworthy. Before getting a reply, he went on speaking.

"Working late again Sage, and on a Friday night too? Aw come on." Kendal teased. Kendal was very caring and if there was no Parker then for Sage it would now have been Kendal.

"Go on you three and have fun for me and you. I'll catch up with you at the festival tomorrow." Sage replied.

She knew that her colleagues, Kendal, Addison and Jay all went to the Hog Wash, a bar just two streets away. It wasn't the most exquisite bar, but the ambience was good. It was plain, inexpensive, clean fun and a great way to spend a Friday night with friends.

However, Sage knew that Parker didn't approve of her going out with her work mates and especially to the Hog Wash Bar. Parker, Sage thought, had 'Champagne taste with a lemonade pocket.' Besides, she certainly had to work; she briefly shut her eyes to block out negative feelings.

Then the door soon closed, and everyone was gone, leaving Sage alone with Jian and the very cold office. Sage knew that Jian made Scrooge look small. He always wore clothes two sizes too small bought in the children's section. Apart from working, his only entertainment each day was to work out how he could spend less. So, the heating went off at its appointed time and it would not be put back on to accommodate her.

Sage now slipped on her coat and settled back in her chair. As Sage's fingers returned to speedily hit the keyboard the noise was not sufficient to cloud out the stifling silence of the room. Sage's mind was also filled with another cloud. It was a constant mass of concentrated worry floating in the air.

This cloud of anxiety was high above the general level of her usual stresses. It was a cloud on the immediate horizon of a big plan which Parker had drawn up to get what he called, financial liberty. Sage was not at all sure about this. He had not disclosed all but the little which was said was disturbing. Sage knew that Parker had never, ever, had any plans, that is, any that worked. Admittedly, Parker was becoming increasingly somewhat irrational in his behaviour, after all, he was in the mix with some 'shakers,' whom he called the 'HLs, i.e., high launderers' so he was bound to get his hands dirty. Regardless, Sage knew that deep down, he really did love her.

Putting these thoughts aside, her mind now rapidly switched back to full concentration of her work. As she persevered with the keyboarding her emotions seemed to keep time with the fast pace of her fingers. At the same time and at a continually increasing rate, Sage felt engulfed by the growing deep silence and calm of the room. It seemed as though the stillness was compressing her thoughts. The office though sizeable, now became a narrow and restricted space which was closing in on her.

Sage stopped and held her head in her hands. She needed a brief respite. Then suddenly, she was jolted from her cerebral gulf by a chilling loud blast which reverberated throughout the room. It was promptly followed by a second, which was just as horrific. These noises appeared to hit and shake every wall as they also echoed deafeningly within her ears. Fear gripped her, as she cowered, ducking low under her desk expecting to be hit by the unseen force which had made the dreadful bangs. Frozen in her terror, she frantically waited but nothing else happened.

After a few seconds of sheer panic Sage slowly raised her head from below her desk. Her heart thumped and her hands trembled. Her eyes almost collided with each other as they scanned the room in double time looking for imminent danger, but she could see nothing, all was eerily still.

Instantly, realizing that the horrendous sounds had come from Jian's office, Sage now flew out from under her shield. She ran the short distance to the office and in a few seconds, she had reached the open door. As she took one step inside, there was yet another thundering noise which shook her entire body. Sage covered her head with her hands. Then, in delayed slow motion, her body coiled and fell limply to the floor.

Chapter Two

When life seems to stop, time still moves and after a short while, blaring sounds of sirens were drowning out the music in the Hog Wash Bar where Kendal, Jay and Addison were enjoying the night. Sipping his Red Leg, Kendal turned to Jay and Addison with raised eyebrows.

"That's a lot of sirens out there. Maybe we should go see what's happening?" Kendal remarked.

As they all looked around wondering what was happening, other patrons were doing the same. Some were moving to the door while others were looking out of the windows.

Addison and Jay looked at Kendal once more but before they could say anything, he was reaching for his coat which was an indication that they should leave. Looking at the customers' exodus the bartender anxiously spoke.

"The police are dramatists they sometimes over play the smallest things." The bartender remarked.

This seemed to be a cost minded effort, to probably stop his patrons from leaving as the bar was not crowded tonight and so sales were not as high tonight so he had to hold on to his few customers.

"In these times, you can't blame them. Let's go see what is happening." Kendal urged.

The three friends gulped and swiftly finished their drinks, then quickly exited the bar, almost rushing over each other. As they hastily walked and reached the street that their office was situated on, they could see and feel the pandemonium which filled the atmosphere. In the distance it seemed like every emergency and police vehicle was present and in large numbers too; from the sounds of things more also seemed to be on the way.

Kendal could see that in this emergency commotion people were moving in all directions. Some were running from adjacent buildings while others were moving to form a curious audience, eager to find out what was happening.

Loud shouts were now filtering out the sounds of the dying sirens as the last emergency vehicle, had now reached its destination.

"Get back! Keep back!" The police officers thundered as onlookers surged forward to get closer looks. Kendal, Addison and Jay, were all part of this flow. The three young friends were swiftly parting human flesh with their shoulders and arms in efforts to get closer to their office building. They had to find out what was going on.

"Sorry, excuse me, please let us through." Kendal offered apologies and demands simultaneously as the three pushed forward against the tide of people. Their minds were racing faster than their feet could carry them and each one of them was filled with nervous fear.

At last, the three had reached the front of the sea of people but were immediately stopped by the police cordon. On closer observation, they were horrified to see in the not too far distance, what used to be their office block. The building was fiercely ablaze! The flames were rising into the night as if they were daring the heavens to stop them devouring their office block. With paralyzed stares, the three stood back from the scorching heat as they desperately fought to gain mental equilibrium. Kendal finally managed to summon words.

"Sage and Jian were in there-." He shakily whispered as his voice trailed off. Kendal held his head in his hands, once more temporarily deprived of speech. Jay and Addison looked at Kendal; then in great disquietude, the three hugged each other. Then, slowly releasing each other, their faces were darkened with dismay, tears welled up in their eyes and some flowed down Jay's face.

Their minds were also now filled with concern and distress caused by this unexpected, bad and dreadful situation; their workplace was on fire! Kendal took deep breaths as though to blow and dispel the panic which he felt within and then he spoke.

"We need to get closer to the police to find out if Sage and Jian managed to make it out. Come on, let's move round to the side." Kendal instructed.

The three inched their way through the crowd to get to the side of the building. Their feet were soaked as they stepped in the puddles of water which ran freely from the drenched building. Angry flames still raged unabated as they spewed forth from the roof with hot embers flying everywhere. Soon they were close enough to attract the attention of a policeman.

"Excuse me officer but we all work in that building and we just want to know if anyone was rescued from it? And how did the fire start?" Kendal rapidly threw these questions at the police officer.

"First, since you work in that building can you quickly tell me how many people were in the building tonight?" The policeman asked with urgency in his voice.

"There were only two people in the office when we left this evening." Kendal replied.

"Who were these people, and what is your name?" The officer inquired.

"Kendal is my name. Jian Ling who is the managing director and Sage an employee were the two people left in there tonight." Kendal said.

"Wait here. I will be right back." The police officer ordered as he swiftly walked off to relay the information to the Emergency Team and Fire and Rescue Commander.

Kendal, Jay and Addison waited and watched with intense consternation. Tears welled up in Jay's eyes until she broke out in loud sobs. Kendal and Addison's cold stares beguiled the raging inner turmoil which they were both experiencing as the black smoke bellowed.

In what felt like a powerless effort, Kendal took out his mobile phone and called Sage's number. Jay took out hers and called Jian's. As Addison watched with anticipation, their faces said it all, as they nervously stared at their unanswered phones. The three were now held in a state of great disturbance and uncertainty. Kendal paced on the spot. Jay and Addison just stared blankly at the burning inferno which was once their work place. In what seemed like ages the officer returned, and Kendal asked his question once more.

"Can you please tell us if Sage and Jian made it out?" Kendal questioned.

"We can't give out any information as yet, but we definitely want to speak with all of you. Please come with me to the police mobile unit so that the Inspectors can get your names and more details about this incident." The officer replied.

As they walked, Kendal felt that this was not the first answer he and the others were seeking. Sage was a young mother with two small children. She was vibrant and full of life. This just couldn't be happening to her and her family. Kendal inwardly felt.

Kendal shifted his thoughts to Jian, their employer. He felt that Jian was an unknown quantity. No one knew much about him but still, he must have a family who cared about him. How did something like this happen and so fast? Just a few hours ago he was joking with Sage, but the hands of time had now rapidly switched the dial to disaster.

Still deep in thought Kendal's senses were becoming numb and Jay had to elbow him to get him to walk faster as the officer pointed to the police mobile unit. As they approached it, the door swung open to allow them entry. The three troubled souls slowly climbed inside.

"I'm Detective Inspector Landry and this is Detective Inspector Riley. We are in charge of this investigation." Detective Landry informed.

He next thanked and dismissed the police officer who had brought the three to the mobile unit. The three young people slowly took the seats which were offered as their legs were like their minds, drained of strength by this terrible situation. They were struggling to comprehend all that was taking place. Everything seemed to be pulling them along before their minds had time to take in these grave events.

"First can you please tell me your names and employee status with your company, All Wired Up?" Landry asked.

The three identified themselves and their posts as bloggers and review writers. The Inspectors took note and Riley responded with a bit of wry reasoning.

"Could this be someone who is disgruntled with one of your reviews?" Riley asked.

"I don't know." Kendal replied.

Shaking this question off, Kendal was not deterred, and he asked about Jian and Sage once more. Again, he did not get an answer but rather another question.

"Can you confirm the number of people who were left in the building this evening?" Riley asked.

"Only two, Sage and Jian who is the managing director." Kendal softly answered.

Just then Landry touched the display screen in the police vehicle and in a few moments the company's name appeared on the screen, with the name of the managing director as Jian Ling along with a photograph. The three peered at the screen as Landry watched them.

"Is this your employer Mr. Jian Ling? And was this man the second person in the building this evening when you left?" Detective Landry inquired.

He looked at the faces of the three young people whose eyes were fixed to the screen display. Landry was awaiting an answer but was interrupted by knocking on the vehicle's door. Riley quickly opened the door and was confronted by a volley of questions. A news reporter had managed to break the police cordon and was throwing rapid-fire questions at the detective. The three started sweating as they listened.

"Is it true that there has been at least one known fatality here tonight? Can you confirm the identity of the individual?" The reporter asked these questions in fast succession as he put his foot in the doorway.

"I cannot confirm nor deny anything. This incident is still under investigation. As soon as we have gathered information it will be released." Riley curtly replied.

He then gently pushed the reporter's foot out and closed the door. Landry then turned his attention back to the three young people and resumed his interrogation.

"Now can anyone of you verify that, that, photograph is Mr. Jian Ling, your employer? The other person left in the building with your colleague Sage?" Landry asked once more. He looked at the three as the wait for an answer became extended.

The mobile police unit became filled with a mind vortex of swirling surprise and unsettling thoughts. Kendal, Addison and Jay were all caught in it. The three could not decide which was more disturbing, the news from the reporter about there being a fatality and not knowing if it was Sage or Jian that had died.

Or the fact that the photograph which they were now looking at, with the name of Jian Ling, was bringing countless questions into their minds. None of these choices were any good for relieving their anxious minds from these alarming events.

Landry waited for an answer from the three as both he and Riley intently watched them, but a great volume of uncertainty and shock was bearing down and settling on the three friends. Kendal looked from Addison to Jay and clearly agony and confusion were keeping everyone's company right now. What was really happening? Then, Kendal sat upright and spoke through quivering lips.

"That person, that face, is not the face of our employer, the man whom we work for, Mr. Jian Ling." Kendal declared.

Chapter Three

In time, the three friends left the mobile police unit, after detectives Landry and Riley had questioned them at length. The three young people had been told to keep themselves available for any further questioning. The strength of their souls was absent as they dragged their feet along the road. The air was thick and dense, and it acted as a heavy burden weighting them down. People seemed to be endless obstacles in their path and weakening their attempts in getting nowhere fast. They had no real idea which direction to turn to, as thinking of Sage and her children, was numbing their minds. Jian Ling or whoever, their now dead employer was, was also yet another confounding mystery that was clouding their thoughts.

Somehow, their wavering footsteps reached the Shard and the three young people, stood opposite, just aimlessly gazing upwards. Kendal thought that life right now was somewhat like this imposing building, standing out against the London skyline and penetrating their innermost being. Life seemed to be demanding more attention, than he could possibly give but he had to be strong for his two friends. He glanced back and could see in the far distance, the smoke and bright embers of their former work place, it was still blazing.

The three walked on and soon reached Embankment; they briefly considered just going to the station but rejected travelling just now. Their footsteps brought them closer to the water's edge and their eyes spotted a small unattended dinghy. They glanced at each other, as the empty little boat seemed to cry out as a welcoming little temporary sanctuary, to rest for a while, to seek peaceful solitude. The three despondent souls, stepped on board, just to catch themselves. As soon as their feet touched the rotten boards of the bottom of the dinghy, it rocked and a drunken figure immerged from under a perished green tarpaulin, barely a gray-haired head poked out. They startled, as blood shot eyes stared at them, but the owner was way too drunk to speak. This long white-haired head, just slithered back under the cracked decaying canvas and continued snoring. The three quietly stood on the cold boards of the bottom of this dinghy, not knowing what to do next. Going home somehow did not feel like an immediate option; they just had to cool their minds before moving a step further.

"Let's just sit for a while, let our minds and bodies catch up with our new reality, he won't mind." Kendal softly suggested as he motioned to the drunken old man in the canvas.

Kendal and Addison gingerly slid to the floor of the boat, trying not to disturb its owner. Jay exhaled but slumped herself closer to Addison who was already opening his coat to let her snuggle inside it. The dinghy swayed from their jolting and the three looked across at the Shard. Kendal thought that its majestic beauty, prominence at being the tallest building in Britain, was little consolation for all that had just happened to Sage. Its towering glass structure however, appeared to offer a glimmer of light, for hope that somehow this tragedy would become clearer, to relieve some of the pain.

They kept still as the boat gently rocked from side to side, with every now and then, the gurgling sounds of the ripples of water, soothing their minds. It was a small comforting respite. Then, suddenly, shattering this stillness, there was a spine-chilling bang followed by an explosion which lit up the entire night sky! It violently rocked the dinghy and immediately, another boom followed, which showered them with glass! The sharp fragments filled and capsized the dinghy!

Gasping for air, frantically bobbing and weaving in the cold water, the three were struggling to stay above the water. It seemed that the sky was raining, piercing pieces of sharp glass! Jagged bits were hitting them in their heads and faces. Kendal desperately tried to pull the drunken sailor from under the water; it was difficult, as he was tangled in the canvas. Jay and Addison tried to help pull him up but as soon as they managed to raise his head to the surface, like a dagger, a huge, pointed piece of glass, fell from the sky and stabbed him right in his left eye! Blood sprayed from his eye, like a burst pipe with a broken stop valve; the three could not contain it. They had nothing to compress it and as the spiky glass daggers kept descending on them, they realized that their efforts to save him were futile. The stabbed old sailor had bled out and they knew that they had to let him go.

Frantically, flailing around in the icy water, they realized that the dinghy was now at the bottom of the river, gone. Kendal, Addison and Jay, were now swimming in the dark, cold, icy, glass filled River Thames! Broken shattered glass and weighty wet blood-soaked clothes, impeded their breast strokes and their adrenaline was heightened in fear of hypothermia. At last, they reached the riverbank, but they were intensely trembling and shaking from the cold water. They wiped their bruised faces and shook pieces of glass from their clothes. Shaking cold water from their ears, they could hear screams and loud shouts which filled the air. They could see people running in every direction as fine pieces of glass which seemed to be filtering through the air was showering them.

The sirens of emergency and police vehicles were blaring but some were grinding to a halt as spiky pieces of glass were bursting the tyres. As the three tried to step and move away, they swiftly looked at the ground they were standing on, and could see that broken shattered pieces of glass, formed a thick blanket covering the ground. Jay tightly gripped Addison's arm and started to cry, while looking at Kendal, whose expressionless face masked his fear.

"Kendal what are we going to do?" Jay sobbed. Addison now hugged Jay as she cried while Kendal searched for words. Kendal too, was in shock but he had to swallow his own dread to create a safe space for his friends. This night had already claimed one of them and so he had to be protective. Kendal clearly knew, that Sage's death represented an enormous tragedy, she was young. This night also just brutally claimed the old sailor but death when old, is like a rite of passage and so it brings a different kind of sadness but not in this case, when these deaths seem so very hard hearted and merciless!

Kendal rested his hand on Jay's shoulder and softly rubbed her arm, while looking directly at Addison, as reassurance that he was still there with them both. Addison released Jay and as the three covered their eyes from the still falling glass, looking around and up, they noticed that the skyline had changed. The London Shard, that majestic, one thousand and sixteen feet, high glass building, was gone!

Chapter Four

After Friday night's horrific events, Saturday morning had arrived, and the detectives Landry and Riley had returned to the Homicide and Serious Crime Division Office. When Landry and Riley left the crime scene of the All Wired Up office, the fire fighters were still not able to put out the fire so it was unsafe to fully examine the building at that point, but it had been left secured and guarded. Then, before they could catch their breath, they had the Shard bursting into flames and the after effects of the glass coating the streets.

Another team of detectives were assigned to investigate the Shard fire and its fatalities. No doubt, these two fires could very well be linked and are possibly, not a coincidence. Although arson was suspected, no evidence of the cause of the Shard fire, was yet clear and no one had claimed responsibility.

On the emotional side of the case with Sage Murphy, the two detectives had arranged with their team to provide a Family Liaison Support Officer for Sage Murphy's parents and her two children. For the interim, this was to be a 24-hour service as they required. Definitive identification of the two badly burned bodies, pulled from the building of the All Wired Up office, still had to be made. Landry and Riley were still waiting on conclusive results from the coroner, for full identification for Sage and the imposter Jian Ling.

Speaking to Sage's boyfriend Parker Davies was their next priority. It seemed clear in these early stages of their investigation that this was a case of a double homicide and arson. What remained puzzling, was the motive. They were hoping to rapidly find this out and apprehend the perpetrators as no one had claimed responsibility for this fire either. Landry and Riley both knew that in a case such as this, everyone was a potential suspect until proven otherwise. They could not right now, jump to conclusions that it was a terrorist attack; they needed proof.

Now sitting in front of their computer screens with cups of hot coffee Landry and Riley were beginning to feel the weight of last night's events but their work was not yet over. The detectives had lots of unanswered questions hanging from high up, about this case. They had received updates that the fire was still raging, and the fire fighters had not been able to put it out, and there was no clear indication of the type of accelerant used.

"What do we have so far Riley?" Landry asked as he sipped and savoured his straight up black coffee.

"Even though no one has claimed responsibility for either fire, are we dealing with terrorists?" Riley queried.

"Two very close building fires-" Landry trailed off.

"We don't want to miss the obvious, but we have Jian Lin, the managing director of All Wired Up, as an imposter but for what reason? His name is not on our radar either." Riley stated.

"We have worked murder and arson cases before, but this one somehow seems different and the Shard, close on its heels?" Landry queried as he finished his coffee.

"We have two victims unrecognizable from burns, with deep penetrating holes in their bodies." Riley stated.

"I just ran a check on the boyfriend of Sage Murphy, Parker; he is no choir boy. Thirty-five years old. Maybe he felt that Jian and the young Sage were getting it on." Riley supposed and continued.

"You know, the boss employee thing. Young woman with too many working late excuses in order to smooch with the boss?" Riley speculated.

He made a second coffee on the heels of the first which he had consumed in a flash, and then pasted the floor with his cup in hand. Landry now kept looking at his screen and then he spoke.

"Sage didn't join the 'Order' either. She's got a runway of debts which a Boeing 747 could comfortably land on, with additional space to spare. But then, possibly Parker and Jian had some shady deal swinging, that went really bad." Landry speculated.

"Parker, yes Parker, is on my radar but could it be a crime of jealous rage about cheating, just maybe?" Riley asked.

"Then torch the place to cover it all up?" Landry alleged.

"Then what about that Jian Ling? Who is the real Jian Ling?" Landry inquired.

"Looking through the details on the man named Jian Ling, curiously enough, his name means 'double edged sword.' Maybe this imposter fell on the real Jian Ling's sword, with a possible business or otherwise criminal deal gone badly wrong?" Riley questioned.

"But why kill the girl if it was business revenge, what part of this puzzle does she fit?" Landry queried.

"Maybe she was in the right place but at the wrong time." Riley reasoned and continued as he made a third coffee.

"This puzzle, the pieces we have somehow do not belong to it. I think that we need to find the right colour and size pieces and we don't have a clue yet." Riley said.

"Well, I have our team trying to trace who the real Jian Ling is and also his dead impostor." Landry explained.

"We must get all the CCTV coverage of that street to see who went in and who came out of that building, not much left of the inside." Riley said and picked up his phone.

"Sergeant Grimes please get us a copy of the CCTV footage of the external office of the All Wired Up company, for Friday, starting from the morning to right through to Friday night. Thanks." Riley requested and turned back to Landry.

"We must also further examine all of those employees, their connections-." Riley was outlining but just then his telephone rang interrupting him. He impatiently answered the call.

"Hello, Detective Riley speaking. Oh, hello again." He said and then listened intently.

Landry watched as Riley's face seemed to be going through different states of astonishment and bewilderment. Landry looked on in curiosity, as he could tell that this was not a personal call but wondered what exactly it was all about, as Riley was looking drained with uneasiness.

Riley's ear was glued to the conversation, Landry started to yawn. They both had grown quite accustomed to sleep deprivation but were always skilled at pressing on with the work. This he would do, as Riley was on the phone. He would run another check on the real Jian Ling. However, he abruptly paused as Riley spoke into the phone.

"I can't imagine it, even if I tried. Have you called in all the necessary environmental services?

We'll be right over. Thanks." Riley said and disconnected the call.

He looked at the expectant Landry who was waiting to be filled in on the conversation which from the sounds of the bits Landry overheard, appeared extremely concerning.

"That was the Fire Chief. We are needed pronto back at the crime scene; other units are already there." Riley hurriedly stated as he stood and hastily put on his coat. Landry speedily rose from his seat and did the same but wondered what had happened to prompt this frenzied urgency? Riley was ignoring everything and reaching for the vehicle keys like a man possessed. In his haste, he was stumbling over chairs as he tried to leave the room.

"What's the update? What is going on? What did the Fire Chief tell you?" Landry asked as he rapidly towed behind Riley.

The haste Riley was moving at, created wind from his swishing coat which ruffled papers on the desks in the office, as he winged pass. All the other officers walking by, looked on in surprise as Riley rapidly straddled the winding stairs to exit the building, through long strides down the stairs taking on four steps at a time and almost knocking aside anyone ascending, Riley suddenly stopped and turned, which made Landry come face to face with him in an almost two-man pile-up.

"What the hell is going on Riley? Bloody hell, what did the Fire Chief say?" Landry demanded.

Riley's eyes widened and then narrowed, as he stared at Landry before speaking. He was out of breath, as his words rolled out his mouth, accompanied by big gasps of astonishment.

"The Fire Chief said that the burnt-out building which housed the company, All Wired Up, no longer exists!" Riley hurriedly explained as another report was coming in on his phone.

Chapter Five

During this chilly morning, it was now 9:30 am; sleep had been an absent guest and misery had taken its place. The day's weather quite aptly reflected Kendal's feelings. He was cold and dead only his heart had not stopped. Kendal had not slept after reaching home around midnight; he remained awake wrestling with the terrible events of Friday night. He felt like an empty jar on a shelf, still holding his form, with nothing left inside.

All this was really too impossible to believe. The news reports after midnight had confirmed that the two badly burned bodies pulled from the office, were suspected to be those of Sage and Jian. His thoughts right now were a deep cold and racing river, coursing through his entire being. He had known Sage almost all his life. They had gone to school together and both liked each other but for some reason, they never made it together as a couple. His parents liked Sage and hers seemed to like him but from them, he had sensed a negative subliminal undercurrent which possibly was the reason that he and Sage never really got together.

Looking back through the years, Kendal was not at all sure if Sage had a life dice which she played. Undoubtedly her life had, had, numerous jostling positions and it had generated random boyfriends. The result of the roll of her dice determined the way she behaved and the choices which she made. This gamble had definitely created uncertainty in major aspects of her life. For sure, it seemed that she had been throwing her dice in a big gambling game of craps, with the boyfriends she had been involved with.

Undoubtedly, now with the man, she had been in love with. The man everyone knew only as Parker. Sage, Kendal felt, was continually manipulated by boyfriends. Unfortunately, she ended up as a single parent. Then Parker came on the scene, a man eleven years her senior with a big habit, big taste and big-time unemployment! Sage was somehow mesmerized by his handsome looks and his pretentious refinement.

Turning over in his bed, Kendal sighed and channeled his thoughts to the good times he had shared with Sage. He wanted to sift out only the quality memories of her. He would frame these and hang them on the walls of his mind. As he thought about this, a tear fell from his eye. He fought to hold back the deluge, but it descended onto his pillow. Suddenly in his disconcerted state, he heard a loud knocking on his bedroom door.

"Kendal! Kendal!" His mother's voice frantically called out.

"Kendal! Wake up! Come on son. Come quickly!" His mother called again.

"OK mum, I'm coming, just a minute." Kendal replied as he wiped his eyes. He guessed what the urgency was and hurriedly slipped on some clothes. As he opened the bedroom door, his mother grabbed him by the hand and pulled him down the stairs as fast as she could get him. Reaching the sitting room, she picked up the remote control, pressed the play button and resumed the news which she had paused. They both stared at the television as the news presenter started to speak.

"We have just received reports that London Bridge has had an explosion and is on fire." The presenter stated.

Kendal and his mum's eyes were pasted to the television; the scene was shocking. Bright red flames bellowed from every inch of the bridge, as one explosion after the next, followed. Several unfortunate people caught in the middle, as they were crossing, were grabbing at broken pieces of concrete and twisted steel bars. Cars were also exploding, creating fireballs which were propelled into the air! Kendal watched the deadly inconceivable scene, as London Bridge had graced this landscape for all of living memory. Agonizing screams filled the air and sections of the bridge were giving way with many pieces plummeting into the river Thames. London Bridge, first built by the Romans in 43 AD, was literally falling down!

To provide viewers with a respite from this upsetting catastrophic scene, the news broadcaster interrupted, with another announcement.

"Authorities are also baffled as to what has caused an office building to totally disintegrate, after what seems to be a double homicide and arson incident occurring on the premises last night, of All Wired Up, situated on Fareham Street, which went up in flames and subsequently the burnt structure of the building, has melted and dissolved into the ground.

Similarly, the same has happened to the Shard, its remaining structure has melted-" Kendal's mother pressed paused on the remote for a second time. She looked at him with sadness and complete surprise before she spoke.

"That's where you and Sage work and your other two friends, Addison and Jay. Son this is serious. Who is it that was murdered and the Shard? I went to bed early last night, so I did not hear any news." His mother anxiously stated.

Kendal sat beside his mother. In his own bewildered state, he had forgotten that he had not informed her that Sage was in the office and was dead. How would she take this news, worse, how was Sage's parents taking their news? Kendal slowly thought.

"I am sorry mum, but I did not wake you last night since I did not want to disturb you with bad news so late in the night." Kendal apologized.

His mother's face looked expectantly gloomy as she looked at her son and subsequently spoke.

"Son, we are descendants from a race that only the fittest survived the Atlantic crossing, so you know that we can withstand anything." His mother said.

She kept her gaze fixed on Kendal's face and waited but Kendal was quiet, so she spoke once more.

"We are making it through your father's death, aren't we? So please tell me what happened last night and most importantly who is it that has died?" His mother worriedly asked.

Kendal's father had died just one year ago and this memory of grief was still warm for both Kendal and his mum. Kendal looked at his mum and spoke with sadness as he relayed the previous night's despairing events. His mother stared at him and then tears flooded her eyes. Kendal momentarily left her, to get some tissues and returned with them along with a glass of water. She wiped her eyes, drank some of the water and then hugged her son. Slowly releasing him, she looked at Kendal who remained very quiet.

"My Lord! That poor child! That poor man!" Kendal's mother finally exclaimed.

Kendal and his mum then sat in solemn silence as if paying respect to Sage and the man they knew as Jian Ling. After a little while, they resumed the news coverage.

"Scientists and investigators are on the scene, probing the melt down of the All Wired Up, building and that of the Shard. Police are also keen to speak to Parker Davies. He is asked to contact the police immediately." The presenter firmly announced.

Kendal's mum turned and softly touched him and then she spoke.

"Why are the police looking for Parker?" Lorraine promptly asked her son. Kendal breathed in and then slowly replied.

"I guess that everyone is a suspect especially if they cannot locate you, as may very well be the case for Parker." Kendal said. He was holding back the other terrors of the night which he and his two friends had gone through; he did not want to alarm his mother further.

"How on earth can a complete building melt? Besides, that building was only constructed about two years ago so how could it be so weak to crumble and melt?" Kendal questioned about his office building and went on.

"What exactly do they mean by melt?" Kendal quizzed.

"Well son, everything these days is made fast, cheap and has to be cost effective. Quality is extra." Lorraine reasoned and continued speaking.

"I bet that they didn't even make it in this country. It was probably shipped all the way out here and then they put it all together." His mother believed.

Lorraine looked at her son as if wanting agreement.

Kendal half-smiled at what his mother had said but even though the news was very distressing, he did not want to get his mother on her soap box on issues, so he instantly changed the subject.

"Mum, I have to speak with Jay and Addison so I will shower and get dressed." He softly explained and went on.

"I need them to come over as soon as possible. I must talk with them." Kendal stressed.

Lorraine looked at her son, she knew that he was very close to Sage, and she could see the sorrow resting solidly on his face, He looked aged by it all.

"That's fine son, I will call Sage's parents. My Lord! They must be in absolute agony, and those two little darling children. What a heartbreak!" Lorraine lamented.

"If they need me, I will go round and see them right away." Lorraine said and continued.

"What is really happening, now there is London Bridge on fire? With all those drowning in the Thames. This is very alarming." Lorraine added and went off to telephone Sage's parents.

Before Kendal did anything else, he sent a text to Jay and Addison telling them the time to come round. In the meantime, he went upstairs and got into the shower. As the cool water trickled down his back his whole body felt painful. His head was throbbing with blobs of questions. Where was Parker? Why did the police want him? Could he be responsible for all of this madness? Who really was his employer? What caused this tragedy? Why did the building crumble? The blobs grew bigger and bigger.

Why did it all happen? Why wasn't he, man enough to stand up for loving Sage, regardless of her parents? Why did he not ask Sage to marry him, no matter how her parents felt? If he had, none of this would have ever happened. Why? Why? Kendal's mind was bursting from his piercing self-interrogation and self-victimization.

In an effort to relieve his soul, he turned the cold water tap up to full blast. The icy water fiercely spewed out and the intense iciness, burned his back. He stood still and allowed it to throttle his body. He wanted to freeze time and turn it back. He wanted his body to be cold, to be as chilled as his barely beating heart. He had to find out more. Sage could not just die in vain.

Chapter Six

One hour later, Kendal was opening his door to Jay and Addison. They grouped hugged and sat silently in his sitting room. Then, Addison looked at his two friends and made an observation.

"This is like being ripped apart by a bomb but still alive. You feel the extreme pain but have no ability nor idea of which body part to search for, first." Addison believed, as he continued.

"Is Parker a terrorist in disguise? Could Parker be really responsible? He knew that Sage was working late. He was also very possessive." Addison stated.

"None of this makes any sense but I am not so sure about Parker. Jian, that Jian Ling-?" Kendal trailed off in thought.

"I feel as if we are absolutely enveloped and completely covered by all of this grief and shock. My head hurts." Jay groaned as she held her temples tightly.

"That Parker man, he wasn't a very nice boyfriend and now he can't be found. What's next in this entire catastrophe? Could Parker have been paid to do all of this?" Jay sadly asked.

"What about that hanger-on cousin of his, Mae? She seemed to be his sidekick if in fact, she really was his cousin." Addison commented.

"For the time being, let's leave Parker for the police to find; I am not so sure that he is the culprit." Kendal answered and went on.

"We have to try to make sense of this insane event but then, it is more than just our office building. Sage did not deserve this." He stressed and continued.

"Then, what about the Shard? Is this connected to All Wired Up, and now London Bridge is on fire? No news about any terrorist claims, either." Kendal said and continued.

"First, we must find out who that man, Jian, really was and what he was into. This surely will give us some information into why this all happened, I bet." Kendal reasoned.

Deep down inside he secretly felt that this was awfully horrible, and it was not looking easy at all but he had to try, for Sage's sake.

"Man, Jian spent almost all of his life in that office. He would have come to work even if he was dead. So how will we know where to start?" Addison worriedly asked.

"Yeah Kendal, Addison has a point. Jian was very secretive. He also had that huge almighty safe under his desk, with loads of money in it. This is not a crime caper novel. It is real life, and Sage is dead." Jay cried as her voice faltered through tears.

"Where, Kendal, where do we start? When the entire building is gone?" Addison added.

Without speaking, Kendal watched both Addison and Jay. He waited to allow Jay some time to release her emotions. He watched his friends, and both their faces were rigid circles of agony. After a while, he spoke.

"OK, I know, that we don't have much to go chasing after, but we can't just sit and hope that the police will solve this. We owe it to Sage." Kendal said and went on.

"We owe it to her children too." He softly whispered as he looked at Sage and her children in a framed photo from the side table. Slowly shifting his eyes back to his friends, he listened as Addison spoke.

"Alright we can try to retrace our interaction in the office with Jian, to see what we unknowingly picked up about him, which could be of use." Addison suggested.

"That is a good idea, Addison but this seems bigger than a single man. Look at tall these other explosions." Jay chimed in, as she wiped her tears away.

"Maybe it is someone who had a grudge about the company. You know, anything which we blogged or reviewed? Like the police were suggesting?" Kendal speculated and continued.

In silence, his two friends just stared at him.

"Well, it is a bit of a crazy world, all overstrung about everything and every comment made but I really don't think it has anything to do with our work." Kendal indicated and carried on.

"My gut feeling is on that Jian, well whatever his real name is, even though we have all these other fires." Kendal stated and continued.

"Which are really like terrorists-" Jay was cut off.

"Jian used to go to the Dragon Tooth restaurant in China Town, on Dean Street." Kendal recalled.

"Out of curiosity, how the hell do you know this, Kendal?" Jay asked.

"Well, I used to go out with a girl who worked at Kings, quite near to the Dragon Tooth and I used to go to China Town to meet her. I would frequently see Jian there." Kendal said.

"Well going to a restaurant in China Town is not against the law." Jay said and sighed.

"Well, yeah, but each time I saw him he was in deep conversation with a man that had, like, a ten years' long beard attached to an expression less face, which seemed rather sinister. They always were pouring their eyes over an iPad, never eating." Kendal explained.

"Again, meeting someone for business is not a crime and did you not see the size of Jian? He was so skinny, too cheap to buy food! So, are you not catching at hair?" Jay moaned.

"Straws, straws, Jay, straws." Addison corrected.

Ignoring Jay's reasoning, Kendal pressed on in his persuasion race.

"You are forgetting that Jian is an impostor so whom he meets up with is important and why if this is a terrorist, why torch our unimportant office first?" Kendal specified and went on.

"Somehow I felt that the man Jian was with, was not a patron but more like he owned the joint." Kendal further pointed out and carried on.

"Well, we kinda also know where Jian lived. So, I can go there and have a search around." Kendal said.

"Kinda? Is not definite and the office is all gone so no hope of looking there for any clues, on an address." Addison said.

"I reckon, that doing nothing is worse than trying. We must find out for Sage and her children." Kendal firmly stated.

"For speed and to see what information we can get, we could split up. You two go to the Dragon Tooth and I go to Jian's place." Kendal suggested.

"You do know that the police will be doing the same." Addison indicated.

"Yeah, but I bet it may take them a little while to put Jian at the Dragon Tooth and they are busy looking into all the other fires." Kendal said.

"Going right now may mean, that we get there first and see what gives." Kendal explained.

"Also, I think that Jian lived in a dingy basement flat in Duck Lane." Kendal alleged.

Jay and Addison stared at Kendal in utter amazement of his knowledge of Jian.

"Again, Kendal, how in the blazes do you know all of this?" Jay asked once more.

Kendal's eyes rested on Jay and Addison. Then he smirked before speaking.

"When people are very private, they generally have something to hide. This secrecy then, becomes a challenge to determine what it is that they are hiding." Kendal remarked and continued as the two kept staring at him waiting for a complete explanation. He blinked his eyes in embarrassment.

"If you must know, one day when I was in his office, he had a letter opened on his desk and I simply glanced at the address." Kendal matter- of-factly said.

"That does not explain how you know that it is a dingy place." Jay stated.

In exasperation, Kendal impatiently reached for his phone. He called up Google Earth and tapped in the post code which he had seen on Jian's letter. He then turned the phone screen so that Jay and Addison could see the street view.

"Now do you see what I mean? And if you look very closely, that looks very much like a woman bending down to take something from out of a plant pot." Kendal pointed out.

"Now we can maybe reason that, just maybe, what she is taking out is a key?" Kendal feverishly asked and went on.

"Those who are very private and think that they are smart, do slip up every now and again." Kendal pointed out.

"So, if we go there, we may get lucky and a key may be waiting for us." Kendal added and went on to urge his friends.

"We have to do this, so let's go. You two hit the Dragon Tooth and see what gives there." Kendal instructed.

"In the meantime, I will check out Jian's Duck Lane address. We have to find Sage's killer." Kendal stated with anger in his voice.

He looked at his friends and hoped that he was right. As they got off the sofa, Jay held back Kendal's hand. She turned to look at him with pain in her eyes and then she slowly spoke.

"I know what Sage meant to you Kendal but wait one minute. I don't have to remind you, but I think that you need to bear in mind, one important thing." Jay anxiously said.

She paused as both Kendal and Addison wondered what she was on about and their puzzled faces stared at her for a fuller explanation.

"If you find this key to Jian's place you can, not only be arrested if you get caught going into his residence but just one look at you, will be all that it takes to possibly shoot you, for breaking and entering. Why not let Addison go there instead?" Jay worriedly indicated.

Addison and Kendal smiled as they now understood what she meant. She did have a very real and valid point. Kendal was fully aware that, not by his own choosing, he had a lot which could possibly go against him. He lightly rubbed Jay's arm to reassure her that he would be careful.

"Luckily Jay, in our country I will only get the taser and not be promptly shot, so please don't worry." Kendal briefly joked. This light hearted humour brought small smiles to their faces, but fear was very much lurking deep within their hearts.

"Kendal, please don't laugh this away. I strongly feel that we all should stick together and go to these places as a team, even last night on the boat, signals that we must be careful." Jay worriedly insisted.

"I think so too, Kendal." Addison joined in, in agreement.

"OK, OK, we will stick together. Don't fear, we can do this for Sage." Kendal reassured once more.

Jay and Addison agreed but Kendal inwardly asked himself, if this was confidence or was, he really just trying to soothe the tremendous amount of trepidation which was starting to swamp him.

As they prepared to leave, the midday news was being broadcast. Kendal's mum joined them in the sitting room to listen. To find out if there was any update on the murders and fires. Lorraine turned up the volume on the television and everyone kept quiet.

"In addition to the London Bridge fire, firefighters have been tackling blazes at the Guild Hall, St Bartholomew's Gatehouse, St Bartholomew's Church and two office buildings in the city. The origin of the fires, is unknown but it is reported that both office buildings were occupied at the time and an undisclosed number of people killed, with extensive damage to all the buildings." The broadcaster paused and then promptly continued.

"We have a live update just coming in and we now join Marston Pines at the scene of the Guild Hall fire. Go ahead Marston." The broadcaster said.

"What has happened here today is a dumb-founding and extremely bizarre occurrence. The Guild Hall building, which was on fire, just simply crumbled and melted." Marston Pines informed and handed back to the studio presenter.

"We take you now to fast paced reports coming from the other fire scenes:

"These two office buildings, which were ablaze, have now been reduced to almost liquid mush." The reporter said. The scene quickly flashed to London Bridge and a reporter commenced speaking.

"This is bizarre, section by section of the bridge has totally crumbled and dissolved, firefighters are trying to contain the structure but its dust, is falling into the Thames at a rapid rate!" The reporter stated and handed back over to the station presenter.

"We take you now to the scene of St Bartholomew's Gate House, and St Bartholomew's Church. These buildings survived, the Great Fire of London and the Blitz, but incredibly, both have now also burnt and dissolved, in front of the firefighters' eyes." The presenter continued as all eyes were glued to the television.

"These fires and strange melt down of buildings are very difficult to understand or explain. The police are investigating, and terrorism has not been ruled out, even though no one has claimed responsibility for these fires and mysterious destruction..." The presenter stated and continued the news broadcast.

Lorraine and the three young people all shared the same confounding looks. After a few disconcerting seconds, Lorraine expressed her concerns.

"What is happening here? First, the building where you all worked went down the same way-." Lorraine commented and broke off.

The three young people were held in her suspended speech as they listened to Loraine's continued comments on what was happening.

"Now all these city buildings have done the same, with lives lost. Is this not terrorism?" Lorraine looked around and asked.

The three young people remained speechless. This news was indeed disturbing and was looking more and more as though the fires were all connected. Kendal however, felt that, they just could not sit and wait on the police. They had to try to uncover the truth about Sage's death. It was a mission to undertake in Sage's name and nothing was going to stop them.

They hurriedly put on their coats and left the house with speed.

Chapter Seven

Soon, Kendal, Jay and Addison squeezed their bodies onto the train. It was a weekend and so every crevice of space was filled with human flesh; the city fires were not a deterrent, even though some services were disrupted. A train carriage that had space for twenty, was now filled with around fifty. As the doors closed, Kendal felt that the atmosphere was heavily saturated with emotional but yet rather displaced thoughts of the passengers.

To pacify his hurt and pain, he discreetly glanced around. He could see those whose stares were within, despite outward intent looks at their phones or iPads. These smart devices he thought greatly inspired self-absorption but not happiness. He touched his device in his pocket, but it had little comfort for his aching soul.

His eyes also noticed the numerous cold gazes mixed in with rived up looks, now being tossed about the train. But these outward empty stares, probably masked the torment of the inner souls of these city bound folk. Kendal knew very well, that his own empty stares concealed the suffering which had now taken center stage in his life. It was now making his mind exceedingly leaden; Sage was gone.

Thankfully, the tannoy soon announced their stop. The three desperate friends swiftly disembarked. Rapidly exiting the crowded station, they stopped and paused for thoughts on their approach to this scheme they were embarking on.

"How will we do this? We have no idea what to ask and whom to ask?" Jay sighed.

"Just follow my lead as we play this." Kendal told them.

Kendal understood that Jay was getting upset but they had to remain calm. He, like Jay, had absolutely no idea as to what he would say and do on reaching the Dragon Tooth.

As they now glanced around, every news stand outside the station had been brightly splashed with newspapers with the headline, 'Mystery Surrounds Melted Buildings, possible terrorist attacks.'

While observing these newspapers and at the same time, thinking about this escapade, caused Kendal's anxiety to increase. But the agonizing thoughts about Jian Ling and who he really could be, had to be uncovered if Sage's murderer was to be found. He was also thinking about these new fires and if Parker was covering the first with these, but could Parker be this high level in crime? Kendal briefly inwardly questioned. Hurriedly refocusing on the immediate present, Kendal turned and looked at his friends. They couldn't look worse if you had shot them, and he felt that he looked the same.

"Let's get a move on." He quickly urged.

As they swiftly walked on, fire service vehicles with sirens travelled passed them, stirring excitement in the air. Pangs of sorrow hit Kendal as he remembered Sage's promise of catching up with them at the festival today. A promise that she could not have known that she would never keep; even the festival had been cancelled. Covered by these feelings, his mind was soon jolted as they had now reached the Dragon Tooth. A sign in the window which said, 'kitchen help wanted' caught Kendal's eye.

Kendal nervously stepped inside followed by his two friends and they anxiously looked around. The air was dense with the scent of Dim sum. These bite-sized helpings of food filled the small steamer baskets.

In Kendal's mind they reflected thoughts of being held captive, never to be released, only to be swallowed up and never to be seen again!

The noisy chatter of all the people sitting around brought reality back into focus but the restaurant was small, and Kendal was starting to feel the squeeze of the walls. Not wanting to panic his friends, he darted his eyes around and just then a man approached and stood behind the cash register.

The man had a long beard, measuring a great distance from end to end; it seemed indefinite. He was the same person whom Kendal had previously seen Jian Ling speaking with. Kendal's frantic brain, swiftly turned to immediate action, as words descended to his lips.

"Hello, we were wondering if we could apply for the kitchen help job which you have posted outside." Kendal inquired.

The bearded old man looked at the three, up and down, nodded his head dimmed his eyes and then he responded.

"Ya, Ya. Only want one, not three. Which one want job?" The bearded old man asked as his slanted eyes watched them.

They could feel his penetrating eyes, little squinty, sociopath eyes; as though he had mental telegraphy, searching and connecting with their muddled thoughts. Unmasking and exposing their lies. Fighting these feelings off, Kendal conjured up courage and stepped forward.

"I do. I want the job." Kendal replied. The bearded old man looked at them again as if examining each one in detail, instead of accepting Kendal's answer. He leaned forward more and eyed Jay up and down.

"I hire girl now. I want girl for job. Maybe I take you later but now, girl only." The old man strongly informed.

Jay instantly fell into an acute mental disturbed state. There was an immediate fall in her blood pressure, caused by this sudden emotional stress, brought on by this man's sinister request. Kendal and Addison looked at her.

Jay became cold, her white skin went pallid; irregular breathing, rapid pulse, and dilated pupils, had now all taken up residence within her pale frightened being. Kendal and Addison kept silent as Jay leaned closer to Kendal's ear.

"What the hell are we going to do?" Jay managed to whisper through clenched teeth.

Neither Kendal nor Addison responded to Jay. They had to think, and they had to do it fast.

"Now, no time to waste. Want job, or not, go. Go!" The bearded old man ordered. He then began gesturing for them to go away.

"OK, I want the job." Jay hurriedly said.

She knew that even though she was scared stiff of doing this, she had to. Sage's face was before her eyes and her little children. Both Kendal and Addison were extremely surprise and really were not prepared for this. However, Kendal's mind there and then, did turbo time. They were young enough looking, to pass for college students in need of work experience. He looked the bearded old man straight in the face and held his cold gaze and then he spoke.

"Can I also work here but do it on a voluntary basis to gain work experience?" Kendal promptly asked.

The bearded old man leaned over the counter once more and watched Kendal. Then he turned his eyes to Jay and Addison as though once more he was probing their thoughts.

"What you mean voluntary work?" The bearded old man quickly asked.

"I will do the work for no pay, just to get work experience." Kendal explained.

"She, your girlfriend?" The bearded old man asked with lowered eyes staring right at Kendal. His face was a mixture of undetermined menacing, frigid stares, with lurking hostility covering his powder white eyebrows and greyish white beard.

"Yes she-" Kendal was sharply cut off before he could completely fabricate his reply.

"Then, she too can do voluntary work. All three! All three, can work here for free." The bearded old man declared.

Kendal had severe misgivings about this new inclusive no expense to the business job offer but it was a step into this place and they would try to make it as short a step as possible.

"What's your name and when do we start?" Kendal asked.

The old man turned sharply and squinted his eyes more at Kendal as though he was reprimanding him.

"Boss! Boss! Don worry about name. Its boss. You start now, in kitchen. Do what chef tells you." The bearded old man loudly ordered.

He then removed himself from behind the cash register and promptly marched the three to the back of the Dragon Tooth. Kendal watched this bearded old man as every now and then the old man looked back at them. Kendal's eyes flit in time with the old man's movements. The old man was rolling in the flour of his seventh decade. His white hair and long greyish white beard looked knackered and peculiar. Strands of long white hair also dangled out of his nose as if seeking to be joined to his beard. His mean and cranky inclinations gripped every muscle in his face but he was remarkably sprightly for his age. Kendal, Addison and Jay kept time with him.

Soon his nimble feet stopped and they entered a vast kitchen, where grease seemed to be the decoration of willful intent, for the counters and also for each of the walls. There was a sickly smell which lingered heavily and complimented the pile of what seemed like endless filthy, greasy pots and pans. Coupled with all this, flour had been dusted everywhere.

Two people turned from what they were doing and looked at the bearded old man. Kendal carefully watched them. The older of the two was short but extremely burly and looked as though he could pick you up with one hand and use your body in a Shot-Put event, coming first in that category! He was the Sumo Chef. The younger man looked like a scared stick insect, who wanted to crawl away and hide. He was a 'kitchen hand,' a young DIA, 'do it all' for the lazy Sumo chef.

These two very opposite creatures, now fastened their eyes on this new work force, that would form the chain gang of lard removal. For a time, no one spoke just uncomfortable glances were shared around. Breaking the muted air, the bearded old man now spoke but in his own language.

"使这些三清理在这里食品检查员即将到来." He loudly exclaimed.

The words bounced off Kendal, Jay and Addison, but Kendal thought that he had said, 'work these fuckers off!" As the bearded old man instructed in Chinese, no one knew what was being said, as the chef seem to angrily stare at them while the bearded old man then promptly walked away. The three were stunned by this and quickly wondered what was coming next.

"What the fuck did he say?" Jay whispered as she started to sweat from the heat of the kitchen but more so, from her rising temperature of consternation.

Kendal and Addison looked at her with glances which indicated silence but then Kendal leaned closer to her ear and whispered.

"I have no idea so let's stay cool but very guarded." Kendal very softly said.

Kendal kept looking all around and his eyes soon caught a small notice stuck to a portion of one wall. It had been almost covered up but the protruding end looked governmental and official, he wondered if it was some type of warning to clean up the filthy place.

Looking around more and more, he could see that overall, the kitchen was massive, greatly oversized in comparison to the front which housed the restaurant. But he had no time for these observations to be explored in depth since the Sumo like chef had now walked over to them and handed out aprons.

Next, he gave all of them gloves, brushes, cloths and cleaning agents.

"Work starts here; clean all these pots and pans, then the fridges, hang out all the table cloths over on the rack, scrub the floor..." The chef detailed an inexhaustible list of chores in what seemed like an army of loud commands.

Kendal noted that his English was very good. However, that of the younger kitchen hand was somewhat shaky; possibly because he was so timid and subdued. Kendal tried hard to think of how they would get information or any type of leads in this place.

In quick time they put on their aprons and commenced the work which seemed unending.

Kendal felt that the kitchen was caught in a perpetual cycle of grime, in a bid to completely replace and take over the structure. Soon their cleaning spiral placed them close enough to speak to the younger man, the kitchen hand.

"Hi, I am Kendal, what's your name?" Kendal asked the nervous young man.

He moved a little distance away from Kendal.

"Hum, we don pass names here. Leave personal outside. Boss don like it." The young man replied.

"Man, this is really important we want to find out if you ever heard of a man called Jian Ling?" Kendal asked.

Instantly, the young man's face creased, and uneasiness was now etched on his forehead, right alongside great alarm. He shifted his stick legs with speed and went behind another counter, away from Kendal. Kendal followed and repeated his question.

"Don't say name in here. No names." He whispered as his eyes whizzed around the kitchen and rested on a waiter, who came to collect a meal.

"Why? Please? We desperately need to find out about him." Kendal pleaded.

"Did you hear of the fire and murder last night at All Wired Up? One of the people was Jian Ling and the other was our best friend." He carried on.

"Please, tell us anything you know." Kendal softly beseeched.

With eyes enlarging and dimming simultaneously, the young man pursed his lips as if to emphasize that speaking was forbidden. He then moved away to the next side of the kitchen. Undeterred Kendal followed him.

"Come on man, all I need is some information. I won't involve you." Kendal beseeched once more.

"Please man, have a heart!" Kendal begged.

"Very bad to talk bout man you look for. This place, no mentioning names. Boss very powerful and dangerous man." The young man warned.

"Please, please, our friend had two young children." Kendal appealed and went on.

"If you know anything, please help us." Kendal implored.

The conversation stopped as the chef gave more orders as to other tasks to complete. As they dispersed about the kitchen, in time Kendal was back close to the young man once more. Once more the kitchen hand moved away but again Kendal followed.

"Did Jian Ling have any enemies that you know of and is he connected to the boss?" Kendal whispered as he knelt scrubbing the floor with the young man chopping pork above.

Kendal waited but the young man kept his lips sealed and rapidly moved away once more. Kendal looked over to Jay and Addison and shook his head from left to right. He was starting to feel that all that, they would get from this situation, was enlarged, greased, lubricated lungs and stubbed fingers from scrubbing.

Later in due course, the young man promptly brushed passed Kendal, causing him to feel the pocket of his apron swinging. Kendal touched the pocket and there was a note inside. He kept on with his current task so as not to attract attention but his curiosity was burning. He looked at Jay and Addison and then at his apron pocket hoping that they would catch on.

Kendal then made his way to the sink, flipped up his apron in what looked like efforts to dust it off and hurriedly took the note out, hiding it in the palm of his hand. He held it in the sink while running the tap. His eyes rapidly stared at the words written on it.

'Opn freezr in bck and pull tray to the rit. Jut look oly. Meat me latr at 10 at picdily stasion. Destry afer reeding.' The badly written note read.

Despite the broken spelling Kendal still was able to make sense of it. Was this a setup by this young man or was it a clue to getting information? He was not at all sure but he had to take the chance. Sage's killer had to be found, he thought. Kendal then swiftly wet and tore the piece of paper and forced the shreds down the sink. His eyes motioned to Jay and Addison once more and they moved closer to Kendal as the chef went to speak to a delivery man.

"Got a note. Going at the back." He whispered.

"Be careful." Jay softly urged as she worriedly looked at Kendal.

"We will watch your back. Do it fast!" Addison urged.

Kendal made his way to the back and instantly opened the freezer. He quietly did as the note had instructed by pulling the tray to the right. Nothing happened. He tried once more with more force on the tray and a terrible scrunching noise was heard.

His heart started to beat outside his chest with gripping fear of being caught. He froze and quickly looked over his shoulder but could see no one. Another hard pull on the tray and this time the entire side of the freezer slid to a recess which opened up and all the contents moved inside the recess. He was astounded and just as he was stretching his body to the max, to get a better glimpse of what was further down; he suddenly heard the bearded old man's loud voice!

Kendal's now over heightened inquisitive desires to see more, wrestled with his dread of being caught. Instantly and without delay he hauled his body up and pulled the tray back out, rapidly closing the opening. He promptly walked and resumed his kitchen jobs, just in time as the bearded old man now entered that section of the kitchen. The old man's dimmed grey eyes, looked around at them, with his face wearing an icy and suspicious expression. He slowly stared at them, one by one. The three kept their heads lowered not to catch his gaze, as he was inspecting the clean up tasks. He next shouted to the chef who came over to him and the two carried on what seemed like an angry exchange of words and then he left the kitchen.

Jay and Addison looked at Kendal with relieved anticipation. They knew that Kendal couldn't tell them if he had discovered anything so they had to wait. The young man kept his gaze away and Kendal did the same. Kendal's eyes seemed to hurt from what he had just seen and craved to see more, of exactly what was deep beyond the opening. His eyes were waiting for his brain to explain the mysterious freezer opening. Deep within his mind bright visions of this strange sight, converted his brain to soft elastic which was now being stretched and made longer and wider by the second as to what existed down below.

His thoughts of that secret opening were causing his mind to expand and reach tearing and breaking proportions for an explanation of this unbelievable irregularity. What exactly was being concealed? Kendal anxiously asked himself.

Chapter Eight

Meanwhile, detectives Landry and Riley continued their investigations into the double murder and arson but now, had to connect to the other divisions who were dealing with these other serious fires and fatalities. They were being stretched in all directions and still could not make any headway nor sense to the All Wired Up, murders neither the recent fires. The detectives understood that murder and carnage never make sense but all that was happening, was creating a new dimension to evil and destruction which they just couldn't understand nor stop.

"We have another report of four more city office buildings going up in flames followed by total melt down." Landry declared.

"Luckily no deaths in those, and no known terrorist group have claimed responsibility as yet for any of these appalling events." Riley stated and carried on.

"Then we have the vast fire and melt down of Madame Tussauds, all burnt and melted." Riley remarked.

"These are very strange occurrences and our Environmental Scientists have been called in to work with our Explosives Teams to uncover the type of explosives being used." Riley detailed.

"Which terrorist group would have such powerful weapons or resources to have this kind of deadly and extreme impact? We have never encountered any bomb which could dissolve buildings and leave only molten liquid." Landry stated.

"No type of accelerants neither indeed explosives, have been identified at any of the fires." Riley pointed out and went on speaking. "On another side, we now have a report that Mae Young is missing. She is the cousin to Parker Davies." Riley said as he looked up from his computer screen.

"Parker and Mae are now both missing. Sage, Parker's girl friend is dead along with her boss. This does not compute at all." Landry said.

"Well, the team did make some progress. The real Jian Ling is living and working a paddy field in faraway Asia." Riley detailed.

"With no possible fingerprints from the burned remains of the man who posed as Jian Ling, identification will take time. The Jian Ling impostor appeared to be a phantom." Landry said. The two detectives did not like this lingering uncertainty.

"We have very little to go on and very much to work through especially with these recent arson incidents and melt down." Riley detailed.

"I sent some of our team over to Jian Ling's, well the man we know as Jian Ling's house but they came back empty handed." Landry said.

"Let's head over there now and see if we have any better luck at finding anything. On return, we need to speak again to the Arson Squad on these fires. Also, the CCTV footage, we need that report from sergeant Grimes." Riley said.

"There has to be a link somewhere from these fires to the first murders." Landry asserted as he looked at Riley in total exhaustion and bewilderment.

Once more the two detectives took their coats and started to leave but as they were walking through the office, they heard their names being hastily called by a frantic officer.

"Detective Inspectors! Landry! Riley! Reports are now coming in, that Tower Bridge is on fire!" The officer spluttered as he delivered the information.

Landry and Riley turned to listen but could not quite believe their ears.

"Please repeat that news? What exactly did you just say?" Riley anxiously asked.

"We have a confirmed report that Tower Bridge is on fire and right now an incoming update that it has totally disintegrated and melted! Sir." The officer heatedly informed.

This alarming statement echoed through the Homicide and Serious Crime Division Office. Barely overcoming this horrible news, Landry and Riley bolted down the stairs. They had to get to the scene and they had to do so with whirlwind speed, maybe, just maybe a new lead my emerge. They had to find some small shred of evidence as to the author of this deadly destruction.

Chapter Nine

Five hours later back at the Dragon Tooth, aprons were hastily shed as the three had now ended their oily tour of duty. Kendal, Jay and Addison were shown out through the back exit by the chef who hastily inquired when they would be returning to complete the cleaning, after all that work and the place still required more cleaning. Giving no committed answer, they just stared around the back and then they bolted down the street.

Out in the open air their lungs now started to recover from the pungent smell of the Dragon Tooth's greasy odours. But the city was now flooded by a mass of people heading in all directions seemingly to escape disaster.

Kendal, Jay and Addison, had been deeply buried in grimy work, for many hours and so they had no idea as to what had recently happened. They listened as shouts rang out in what seemed like fearful expressions.

"What's happening?" Jay asked.

"Jay we are in the same canoe as you, just keep moving." Kendal urged and went on as the briskly walking people seemed to be pushing them along.

"Something has happened at Tower Bridge that much I understand." Kendal informed.

His legs were moving fast but his mind was bursting with what he had seen inside the freezer of the Dragon Tooth. As he rapidly walked, it all started to flow out.

"You won't believe what I saw." He hurriedly said as he stepped with fast and deliberate strides, looking sideways at Jay and Addison while avoiding fast paced walkers. Jay stepped up her stride to keep pace and then her anxious question came.

"Come on tell us we are dying to hear everything about the suckling pigs which you found in that back freezer. Knowing our luck, bet that was all there was." Jay pessimistically teased.

"We need to get inside a store with a café, shops are still opened, so I can tell you privately." Kendal hurriedly said.

He was out of breath from the speed they were walking at, putting distance between them and the Dragon Tooth was a priority. He felt edgy, anxious and extreme nervous curiosity, all at once. He started to look all around, ensuring that no one was following them as no one could be trusted from the looks of that old man and the chef.

In a matter of minutes, they had reached a store and rushed inside. Taking the escalator, they ran on the moving steps to reach the landing. As they stepped off, they followed the signs for the store's café. Thankfully, the café was almost empty based on what seemed to be happening outside. They rushed in, out of breath and took seats. Straightaway, Kendal commenced speaking.

"The Dragon Tooth is a front for something but I have no idea what." Kendal nervously declared.

His expectant audience faces, all dropped in disappointed stares. Jay shifted herself into a more upright position and instantly spoke up.

"Do you mean to tell us that we spent an eternity cleaning that filthy place, all for nothing?" She angrily asked.

"Calm down Jay, let Kendal finish." Addison advised and squeezed her hand.

In total resignation Jay drew closer to him and put her head on his shoulder. She then started to cry.

Realising the despair which was spreading, Kendal got up and paid for drinks and sandwiches for everyone. He then placed the items on the table but all appetites were spent. The refreshments remained untouched. After a brief while Kendal commenced speaking once more.

"There is a secret room in the back of the kitchen. It is hidden underneath the freezers and has an automatic opening lever disguised by the freezer tray." Kendal excitedly described.

"That bearded old man is so eccentric that can we not expect that he would have something as weird as that?" Addison asked.

He looked at Jay who was still leaning on his shoulder but she was now crying.

"I could not chance staying to look at what it all really was but I think that we should go back later tonight." Kendal suggested.

Instantly without hesitation, Jay jumped on Kendal. Her eyes were bright red from crying and she was like a ferocious beast defending her life.

"You are losing it Kendal! If they caught us, we would end up on their menu and served as exotic Chop Suey! Jay exclaimed and continued.

"Going back there would be like kissing a fox." She cried and went on.

"Let's just throw this all in and leave it to the police especially with all the other fires, this is getting beyond us." She heatedly added.

"We have come this far, let's not turn back." Kendal coaxed his work worn, tensed friends.

He looked at them sympathetically. They both wore the mask of defeat but Kendal was not giving in yet. He remained undeterred. He knew that he had started this for Sage and he had to finish it; he felt that even it all turned out to be a sick terrorist, he was willing to find out.

"Look, if you want, I will take you both to the train station and continue alone. I don't want you to do anything which you are not happy about and most of all, I do not want either of you to get hurt." He explained.

Jay and Addison's faces were now stark white as they looked at Kendal and then they both looked away, as if giving themselves one more chance to think this dangerous pursuit over. After a few minutes Addison rubbed Jay's shoulder and then he looked at Kendal.

"I'm still in with you." Addison assured but he kept rubbing Jay's shoulder hoping that she would come around but would understand if she wanted out as this was not simple and was becoming very involved.

After a while, Jay dried her eyes. She sat up and shook her hair back as both her friends waited for her to speak. Then, she looked at them and gave a little smile. She was feeling extremely stressed but did not want to let the others down, after all, Sage was her very good friend.

"OK, me too. I am with you Kendal." Jay resignedly whispered.

She then rested her head back onto Addison's shoulder. Addison could feel the softness of her hair and it sure felt good after all they went through today; it was refreshing to feel its softness.

Kendal looked at his two friends and wondered why they too had never gotten together. He knew that they liked each other but like him, both had no emotional attachment to anyone. Why had life, he wondered taken him, Sage, Jay and Addison from one uncomfortable place to another. Allowing them to just shift between them but never seeming to settle or move on.

Anyway, snapping from his thoughts he thanked his friends and started outlining their next moves. His senses felt stirred to action by what he had seen in the kitchen.

"I forgot but that young kitchen hand also asked me to meet him at Piccadilly Station at 10 tonight." Kendal informed.

"Just maybe we can get some real information. He acted very mysteriously especially when asked about the bearded old man and Jian Ling or whoever he really was." Kendal outlined as his two friends listened.

"Next move boss?" Addison smiled but anxiously asked while trying to disguise the apprehension which he felt.

"We have four hours to kill before meeting that guy so I suggest that we go to secretly check out, Jian Ling's address now." Kendal replied.

The three rose to leave and Jay put the untouched refreshments into her backpack. As they walked out of the store's café, they were within the household section where they overheard a disgruntle customer having an argument with staff at the customer service desk. They could clearly hear the exchanges.

"I showed you the receipt of having purchased this set of items from your store. So, I want a refund for this defective cooking set." The woman argued.

"Madam, we would happily give a refund if we saw the defective set but all you have is a bag filled with molten material." The store rep countered.

"I told you I bought the set of saucepans from here just last month. This morning just suddenly the box burst into flames. My husband threw it outside and very soon, everything in the box had melted!" The customer described.

The argument continued growing louder and more intense. Kendal, Jay and Addison walked on.

They had their own troubles with no end in sight but they all thought that it all was very curious. Addison looked back at his friends.

"Possibly a scam? Saucepans bursting into flames and melting? Are people getting creative, based on the buildings melting?" He remarked.

"People try anything nowadays. Buy clothes, wear them out to their special occasion, then carry them back to the store and get a refund, saying that they didn't fit or some other lame excuse." Jay pointed out and went on speaking.

"I've seen it all; remember I used to work at John Lees. The fake and the pompous all do it too. So, she probably melted down the saucepans herself! But still a bit farfetched-" Jay remarked and shrugged off the overheard conversation.

Shelving this passing incident, the three exited the store and headed to get a bus for the journey to Jian Ling's house, even though they could walk to it, they were tired. As they approached the bus stop on the other side of the street, the small bus shelter suddenly burst into flames, sending bodies wildly into the air.

The explosive shockwave knocked the three friends to the ground as the dust engulfed them. Kendal struggled to be free from the stifling particles. Slowly he rose to his feet and started to look around, dazed and blurry eyed, his thinking was unclear.

Addison scrambled up from in the dust and Kendal now managed to recover, stood and dragged Addison free. They both madly searched about in this clouded air, for Jay, as the dry powdery eruptive mist was both stifling and blinding. All they could feel was tiny particles of earth and waste matter which were lying on the ground and also carried in the air. Their minds were shattered as they coughed and spluttered in their feverish efforts to find their friend.

"Jay! Jay! Jay!" Both Kendal and Addison cried out.

Frantically bending over groping, searching blindly, by feeling with their hands, finding other dead people but not finding Jay. Kendal ran with a barely breathing child in his hands and passed her to a store worker. He then returned and joined Addison in the search for Jay. They screamed her name but got no answer. Their hearts beat with dismay and their hands fumbled about in the dust. Finally, they found Jay. Addison swiftly lifted her into his hands.

"Jay! Jay!" Kendal called out and slapped her face as they hurriedly carried her back into the store. Store workers were forced into action, they were running everywhere with first aid supplies and Kendal stopped one to help with Jay.

Addison placed Jay on a chair. As the emergency first aid kit was snapped opened.

"Jay! Jay!" Addison and Kendal repeated her name but Jay's eyes remained closed, with no response from her soul.

Chapter Ten

Big Ben struck eight and the hour found the city with police specialist operations, fire and emergency services on high alert. The city it seemed was under siege. Saturday night, revelry had been cut short and people were asked to make only essential travel.

Landry and Riley were once again sieving through the reports which they had. Unfortunately, these all remained reports more so than evidence. They had nothing to go on and the threat level could very well be raised to severe. The Cobra Committee and the Prime Minister had been informed.

"What do we have or what is it that we should have but don't?" Landry asked and carried on.

"Tower Bridge wiped out completely! Melted! The number of city office buildings has risen to twenty. Twenty bloody buildings, gone! All melted. I never thought it possible that a building could dissolve but here we have it, liquefied." Landry lamented.

"A bus shelter wiped out and melted, more fatalities. Is this a random mad man we are searching for? Rather than organized attacks?" Landry asked in a perplexing tone.

"The Bomb Squad, sent over CCTV images from the bus shelter scene and the Shard." Riley said.

"And? Landry asked.

"Guess, what? Images of those three young people, from the All Wired Up office, places them walking around the Shard last night and also by the bus shelter today." Riley stated and reached for his phone.

"Grimes come in please." Riley called out to the sergeant.

Soon there was a knock on the inner office door and sergeant Grimes came in to join Landry and Riley.

"Can you please run us through the CCTV footage of the street and entrance of the first company to go, All Wired Up, bloody strange name." Riley grumbled.

"Those three, need to be spoken to again, I'm not trusting them right now." Riley stated.

"Not to mention, their mysterious business employer and yes, Parker, can't shake him away either as there is still no sign of him, so what part does he have in this?" Landry added.

The sergeant called up the footage and projected the video onto the wall screen. The officers watched as people went in and out. This was as exciting as watching paint dry, Riley thought, but nothing appeared out of the ordinary.

"No one else went in or out apart from those who worked there." Sergeant Grimes fully explained.

Landry and Riley kept looking at the CCTV footage, hoping to see anything which could indicate that something was wrong or inconsistent. They could see nothing but the people who all had a legitimate right to be entering or exiting the building and flickers of probably wind blowing.

"I want a cleaner image of the man who called himself Jian Ling. We need to circulate that image wider a field than this country." Riley requested.

"Riley, I spent the entire day on the footage and there is nothing else that I can do to the get the image any clearer." Grimes said and went on.

"There seems to be a mist over his face, almost like a shield and there are some days that he never entered nor existed that office." Grimes explained.

"There is nothing else apart from that, which indicates any irregularity whatsoever." Grimes stated.

Landry and Riley played back section after section of the CCTV footage despite reassurance from sergeant Grimes. They both felt that something was not right. After several minutes Riley spoke.

"OK but-" Riley was cut short by his ringing phone. He anxiously reached for it but each time it dropped back onto the charger. Riley finally grabbed the phone with worried energy and placed it to his ears.

"Yes, Riley speaking. Oh, hum, are you absolutely sure? Are the tests conclusive?" Riley asked and went on.

"Well, that is at least some kind of break through." Riley paused and went on.

"Thanks, will get back to you." Riley said and ended the telephone conversation.

Landry and Grimes watched as Riley held the phone in his hand as if he was holding on to evidence.

Riley next turned his attention to Landry and Grimes who were waiting to hear what the conversation was about.

"That was the coroner." Riley said and stopped as he looked at both men in pensive thought with the phone in his hand.

"Riley, you have a way of using verbal torture to inflict punishment on colleagues." Landry accused and carried on.

"Get on with it. Tell us what the coroner said." Landry ordered.

"The two charred bodies pulled from the All Wired Up, burnt out and now melted premises, one of those-" Riley abruptly stopped again and looked at his notes while swinging the phone.

"For Christ's sake! Riley, get on with it, you verbal persecutor!" Landry joked.

Landry couldn't stand the suspense. Sergeant Grimes kept silent. Everyone expectantly watched as Riley shook the phone in his hand several times and then returned it to its charger. He once more looked at his expectant colleagues and then he spoke.

"One of the bodies, the male, from the All Wired Up building, is that of Parker Davies, Sage Murphy's boyfriend. Parker is the dead male." Riley surprisingly revealed.

Chapter Eleven

Time had moved deliberately slow after the bus shelter explosion. They had kept well out of the way of the swarm of police after the maddening incident. Kendal felt that it was so remarkable how time becomes very sluggishly slow, when dismay lingers. It was now 8:45 pm and they had shelved the plans to go to Jian Ling's place, actually the bus shelter explosion had made that decision for them.

In Kendal's mind he had no answers whatsoever about all that was happening. The All Wired Up fire, followed by all the others and the murders. After all he was not a trained detective, not even a police officer and what if he stumbled on a real-life terrorist? How would he manage? He questioned himself, but then again, terrorists are really mere cowards, who hurt innocent people so he could handle this, he worriedly self-assured.

Then, perhaps what was happening was just a case of bad chance that all these fires or rather explosions were occurring at the same time as Sage and Jian's murders, and they were all just a sick coincidence.

Still, entire buildings bursting into flames and melting? First, starting with their office, All Wired Up, and now so many others? Kendal could not stop thinking, his mind was a mess; maybe it was time to stop. Jay was probably right and he was too stubborn and determined, resistant against all sensible advice; he inwardly reasoned. Luckily Jay had responded well to the first aid treatment and her blood circulation and breathing had been restored. The entire experience was extremely frightful and serious. If they had been nearer the bus shelter, Kendal didn't think that, they would have been alive right now because many others had been killed.

He and Addison were completely shattered and despondent but yet overjoyed that Jay was going to be OK and so they had decided to give Jay a chance to fully recover by checking into a small B&B.

Both Kendal and Addison had called their respective relatives to reassure them that they were safe and would be home soon. Jay had grown up in foster care and was practically a loner; apart from being with them, she had no one else.

Jay was asleep now and Addison was watching over her. He was also keeping his eye on the news of what was now suspected to be the terrorist attacks in the city. Kendal looked at his watch. He had one hour and fifteen minutes before the scheduled meeting with the young man from the Dragon Tooth. He would do this alone, leaving Addison to watch out for Jay.

He now directed his gaze towards the small window. The glass pane seemed to have the imprints of earlier faces like him he thought, seeking release from a troubled soul. He wiped the glass and could see from the darkened skyline the city in a distorted view; it seemed as though it was looking from a prism.

Everything appeared as though it had refracting surfaces separating the white street lights into a spectrum of dark melancholy colours, as the light bounced from the black silhouetted buildings. Without the noise of the traffic and the buzz of the people scurrying along, Kendal felt that the city now seemed bitterly unwelcoming and foreboding with all that was happening within it. At last, it was time to leave. It would be a five minute walk to reach Piccadilly Station. As he put on his coat, Addison looked up and spoke.

"Got your phone? Take care bro." Addison said as Jay stirred and sat up from the bed.

"What's happening?" Jay sleepily mumbled.

"Rest." Kendal softly replied as he eased closer to the door, hoping that all would be well and that it would be soon over.

"Hey, Kendal, watch out." Addison warned once more. He walked over to Kendal and they fist bumped.

Kendal promptly left and softly closed the door behind him. He speedily made his way to the outside of the B & B. How dangerous can this be? Just meeting with this frightened guy to hear what more he can tell me, Kendal tried to reassure himself. However, deep within, he did feel uneasy and so he placed Sage's face in his mind.

His footsteps increased in haste and soon he was standing outside the station; he pulled his baseball cap lower down on his forehead. People were hurrying in and out but the kitchen hand was nowhere in sight. He looked at his watch and it was now 10:02. He did not want to aimlessly stand outside the station since he would attract the attention of the armed police who were about in full force, given all that was happening.

He nonchalantly looked around, then he walked off to a little distance and paced around the Eros statue on the Shaftesbury Memorial Fountain. As he did this, out of the blue a loud voice punched the air and startled his mind.

"Hey bro! What's the haps?" The voice said.

Kendal then felt a hand on his shoulder. Turning in surprise, Kendal recognized the face; it was Lenny. This was the last person Kendal wanted to see right now.

Lenny was a character who had distinct mental and moral qualities which were like magnets, that attached to the uniform of every city police officer!

"Hiya Lenny. Can't stop to talk right now, busy." Kendal explained, in a hasty effort to lose Lenny.

"Busy my ass! You was just standing here and besides, what you doing down here, when everybody running from the terrorist attacks?" Lenny responded as he looked at Kendal suspiciously.

Kendal was listening to Lenny but keeping his eyes on the station. He just had to get rid of Lenny before the police moved both of them on or the young guy saw him with Lenny and disappeared.

"If you must know, I am meeting a date. Don't you have somewhere to go?" Kendal retorted.

"At this time? Who's she? A street crawler?" Lenny accused and carried on.

"Your mother, Miss Lorraine is a good church going woman, what would she think, Kendal?" Lenny said, in a drooling high pitched mocking voice.

Without answering, Kendal walked off to get back closer to the station. But to his dismay, Lenny followed.

"Wasn't it your one time girlfriend that was killed last night? That, Sage girl?" Lenny probed and continued.

"She should have stuck with you; ended up with that married snob, a shaker and dealer. I can't understand how some women like married men, when people like me and you, ain't married, but free and easy." Lenny glibly stated, all the while smiling.

"What do you mean, by Sage ending up with a married snob and shaker and dealer? Who exactly are you talking about?" Kendal queried.

This was hurting Kendal's head and he had to keep focused for this meeting even though this news about Parker could be useful.

"That jackass, she was living with. That, Parker guy." Lenny said and went on.

"He was bloody married! And the gangs, the shakers and dealers, you know, them, the HLs. The high laundering gangs, and washing is definitely not their business. All them HLs have their hooks in him." Lenny asserted.

Kendal really could have done without this right now but this news could be significant in Sage's murder. Although he wanted to know more, it was now breaking his concentration and so Kendal walked faster but Lenny was on his heels.

As Kendal turned to beg him to go, out of the corner of his eye he could see the young man from the Dragon Tooth hurrying towards the station. Kendal had to rapidly place what Lenny had said about Parker to one side. He then changed direction and promptly started walking to meet the young man. Lenny was still his shadow.

"Lenny! Leave me the hell alone!" Kendal rapidly turned and exclaimed.

He then proceeded to push Lenny back but had to stop as his foot was trapped in a piece of large paper which blew and encircled his trainer. Bending to remove it, pens fell from his pocket. As he tried to retrieve them, by this time, the young man had reached him and the unrelenting Lenny.

Kendal looked up and could see that the young man had the same frightened look as from before. He stared at Kendal and then at Lenny who had a broad silly smile on his face. Lenny's smile turned to speech.

"Oh, I see, I understand now, Kendal! You don't have to worry. I am cool with anything you want to be. So, this is the date you were waiting for, this is the hook up!" Lenny smiled and exclaimed, in total misunderstanding of what was happening. Kendal tried in vain to push Lenny away as the frightened young man fixed his eyes on Lenny, who continued speaking while cheekily smiling at the panicky young man.

"Don't worry man. Kendal will be as gentle as a pussycat with you. You in safe hands, man." Lenny joked as he winked at the young man.

"Ignore him he is an asshole." Kendal said as the young man fearfully watched them both.

"I speak with you alone?" The young man uneasily asked as he anxiously helped Kendal to retrieve the last pen from the ground. He then watched, as the paper which was stuck to Kendal's trainer remained firmly lodged. It was resisting removal as Kendal frantically tried once more to dislodge it and at the same time reassure the young man that they could speak alone.

"Yes, we can go-" Kendal started to say but was instantly cut off in mid-sentence by what felt like a gush of wind swooping pass them. At the same time, the young man lurched forward and Kendal and Lenny quickly caught him.

As they tried to steady him, his legs buckled, and he started to fall. Breaking the fall Kendal and Lenny then positioned him onto the ground. His face was instantaneously being drained of colour and his lips appeared to be rapidly swelling and turning blue.

He had a tight grip on the pen which he had picked up and he motioned in a gesture of wanting to write.

"Just hold on man, we will get you some help!" Kendal anxiously said as panic was setting in.

Lenny was watching the gestures and snatched at the paper, which was stuck to Kendal's shoe, swiftly tearing off a piece.

"Paper? Write?" Lenny asked and held the paper on the back of his hand so that the young man could write. His shaky hand barely had enough strength it seemed, to scribble one word on the dirty makeshift page, before it fell limp. The young man had expired, it would seem. Lenny put his head to the young man's chest to verify what they thought, while Kendal bent over and watched.

In a few seconds Lenny raised his head and in slow shaking movements, from left to right, Lenny's eyes lowered and then he spoke.

"He's dead, man. He's gone!" Lenny said.

Chapter Twelve

Screams, high-pitched, loud, deafening cries, expressing extreme fear and emotion, pierced the night air as two women stumbled on Kendal and Lenny standing over the body of the young man from the Dragon Tooth.

Kendal and Lenny had no time to explain, as six police officers wearing tactical uniform and full-face visors, rushed from the station and wrestled them to the ground.

Kendal sputtered and gagged as he breathed in loose soil and fragments of dust. Lenny knew this drill well and held his breath. His face was close to Kendal's, and he just played dead.

"Ambulance! Quick! This one ain't breathing!" One police officer shouted.

Kendal listened to the commotion and prayed that Lenny wasn't dead. In no time the paramedics arrived and hoisted him onto the trolley using CPR in the process. Very rapidly, Lenny was gone while Kendal faced the dead!

"Up! Up! What's your name?" The policeman demanded.

"Patrick, Patrick Gibbs is my name and I did not kill anyone! I don't even know him." Kendal lied. There was no way right now that he was giving the police his real name or any information about this dead man.

"We are placing you under arrest on suspicion of murder. You have the right to remain silent anything you say…" The policeman read out all his rights and then continued questioning.

"Who is your mate, the one just taken away?" The officer rapidly asked.

"You should go ask him but you probably killed him." Kendal roughly replied. He was attempting to use divergent tactics to get them to refocus off of him for a bit. He felt angry and the tight handcuffs were hurting his pride more than his wrists since there was now an audience, people were gathering.

Clearing his throat and retching from the dust which was hanging about in his mouth, Kendal made the most awful sound and movement of attempting to vomit. The police moved him back just slightly so as to avoid being hit by any imminent spewing.

Kendal bent over and watched as the police were examining the body along with the coroner who had just arrived on the scene. He could hear the coroner as he did his assessment of the body.

"Small puncture in the neck is the most likely point of entry for the poison. Most likely a needle but it looks like a dart, very strange, hum." The coroner noted.

Kendal was pulled back up erect and very soon he was led away to a parked police vehicle. He was searched his pockets emptied and all items confiscated. He was then placed in the police vehicle to be taken to the station.

Kendal's head was spinning as the vehicle roared through the streets. He could not believe that this was happening. Kendal felt that this was like a dream, more precisely an awful nightmare!

In no time, the police vehicle came to a jolting and abrupt stop right behind the ambulance which had just taken Lenny. The ambulance was overturned and on its side. The road was blocked with burning debris and smoke filled the air. The communication radio in the police vehicle was transmitting urgent information.

Kendal strained both his ears and eyes to find out what was happening. Just then, a loud explosion was heard which rocked and lifted the vehicle he was in, into the air. It landed violently on its side. Dazed, Kendal realized that the two officers were thrown out of the car, their seat belts were totally disintegrated. He struggled to push the side air bag off his chest. Just then, the vehicle's door was thrown open. He felt a hand pulling and dragging him out of the car. His chest hurt from the impact but he hoisted and shoved himself to help his rescuer, to pull him free.

Now out from being trapped, through uneven breathing, he looked to thank his rescuer but he was unsteady and slipped, as the loud noise of sirens were blaring in the distance.

"Come on! Man! Move it!" A familiar voice sharply ordered.

"Lenny! Lenny! It's you! You're alive!" Kendal excitedly exclaimed as he tried to touch and grab Lenny on the head and face with his manacled hands. He slipped once more and rested on the ground.

"Hey baby cakes no time for this rosy sentimental greeting. We in the shit and if they catch us again, deeper shit! Move! Get up man!" Lenny swiftly ordered.

Kendal jumped to his feet and started to run but Lenny held him back. Lenny swiftly looked around and then ran over to an unconscious policeman. Kendal ran with his hands still locked together at the front and watched as Lenny searched the police officer for the keys to the handcuffs. He soon located the keys and turned to Kendal.

"He'd be fine just a very bad headache will follow." Lenny pointed out as he unlocked the handcuffs and set Kendal free.

"Thanks man. Thanks." Kendal gladly said.

Kendal then rapidly returned to the police vehicle. He rummaged and searched like a man possessed. His heart started sinking and his eyes grew tired. His stuff which they had taken was nowhere to be seen.

"Come out." Lenny commanded and continued to speak.

"You soft guys, you don't know the street." Lenny laughed.

He then walked to the boot of the police car. He prised it opened and picked the lock of the strong box which they carried all of the confiscated items in. Lenny rapidly snatched his out and moved to one side.

"Here, look and find your stuff and be fast too." Lenny commanded.

Kendal hurriedly dug into the box.

"Got all of it." Kendal piped.

He then filled his baggy trousers' pockets with all of his stuff.

Lenny then once more looked in the full box of the varied seized goodies but resisted the challenge to fulfil his night time dreams. He smiled and just sharply closed the box. Turning to Kendal he directly spoke.

"Phone? Kendal phone?" Lenny demanded.

"What the hell for Lenny? Payment for saving me?" Kendal hastily asked.

"No shit head! We have to take out the Sim cards otherwise the police will be able to track us." Lenny explained.

He rapidly removed his and continued speaking while pulling Kendal's phone out of his hand.

"Simple. GPS man, they watching us all the time but still can't find the fuckers who doing all this." Lenny complained and continued.

"They noted down our phone numbers too. I saw when they took mine off of me, as I lay dead on the trolley." Lenny laughed as he swiftly pulled Kendal's Sim card out.

"Hope yours ain't on a contract for them to get your name and address." Lenny worriedly stated.

Kendal watched as Lenny bent down beside the police car and pushed the Sim cards into the wheel hubs of the vehicle. He then promptly jumped up and dusted off his hands onto the side of his trousers.

"Let them chase their tails with that." Lenny laughed again and then he became somewhat somber.

He looked around in the distance and wiped his face from the dust.

"That was Admiralty Arch that just went up. Two explosions, so it most likely will melt like all of the others." Lenny gloomily reasoned. They looked at each other, as sirens were getting closer and the two ran like the clappers into the disturbing night.

Chapter Thirteen

Midnight arrived and found Addison pacing the floor. Jay had rolled out of one restless sleep right back into another. Addison was glad that at least one of them was temporarily escaping this horrific reality. He looked at his watch once more, worry was setting in. Kendal had not yet returned. The television was now his constant companion but he sharply turned his back on it and looked out through the window.

Addison very well imagined and he thought rightly so, that midnight signaled open season for murder, shakedown, rape and robbery. It meant walking with speed using all round vision, bracing yourself against the inky blackness and praying your number isn't up!

Addison knew that if the gangs and cut-throats have it in for you, then at midnight, it is every man for themselves. Even though with so much trouble all about, these gangs in the city would still prey on any unwitting soul.

Addison was desperately hoping that Kendal's number hadn't been called by anyone of the gangs or by the man he was set to meet. He really should have been back by now and there was no answer from his mobile phone.

"Addison, um, Addison." Jay rolled over and softly called.

"Hey, Addison." Jay murmured once more. Jay's calling suddenly broke Addison out of his brain racking moments.

"Jay, you're awake." Addison responded. He ran over to the bed and hugged her. They embraced tightly as once more her curled brown hair danced in between his cheek and shoulder so that her hair hung in more waves than curls.

He softly caressed her, rubbing her back then kissing her head. As he slightly moved her, to look into her eyes, this tender moment was interrupted by the scene which was spread across the television screen. They could visibly recognize people in the news bulletin. Quickly, releasing each other, Addison raised the volume of the television.

"The police are seeking two men in connection with a murder which occurred just after 10 pm on Saturday night, just a few metres from Piccadilly

Station. They both escaped police custody and have not been seen since. Police are also keen to speak to these two men about the recent explosions occurring around the city." The broadcaster said and carried on.

"These images of the two men were released from street CCTV…" The broadcast continued but Addison and Jay were unable to comprehend any of what else was said. Their eyes were immobilized on the images which were bold and clear, one of Kendal and one of Lenny!

Addison and Jay both looked at each other. Shock was becoming a habit but they couldn't hold back the enormous and incredulous expressions which blasted out from their faces.

Their eyes now swiftly expanded to the limits of their sockets and their hearts pumped with resounding fearful rhythms.

Finally, Jay seized her lips and they parted to allow her to speak.

"This is going from bad, straight to absolutely hopeless!" She cried out and continued.

"Kendal! Lenny! How? Why?" Jay exclaimed, as she held on to Addison in downright despair.

Chapter Fourteen

Sitting on the bed and rocking back and forth Jay took turns between swinging her body and crying. She was beside herself with fear and desperation.

"What are we going to do now? First Sage and Jian or whoever he was, are dead. Now Kendal is wanted for murder but how did Lenny get involved in all of this?" She cried.

Addison shook his head without responding. He too had no answers and was now contemplating their next move. What really, were they going to do? Addison inwardly asked himself.

As he looked at Jay, there was a rustling of the door lock. The two froze and waited. In Addison's mind it could be the police coming in to get them since they were all linked to Kendal, Sage and Jian. He braced himself for the worse.

The door slowly slid open and very quietly Kendal's head appeared as he then allowed his entire body to step inside. Jay and Addison both got up and ran to him but stopped as a shadow appeared to be moving and pushing Kendal further into the room.

Kendal swiftly moved aside, and in stepped Lenny. All eyes were now fixed on Lenny.

The room went hushed apart from the loud heaving coming from deep within their chests. It was their weighted breathing which the three friends were producing at a high rate. If they looked closely, even the windows were clouding over from their breath.

"Hey what's with all this heavy breathing? This ain't an obscene phone call. It's me! Lenny." He said breaking the huge silence.

Kendal waited for the flurry of questions from his friends but none came. They just stood with panicky stares. He sank onto the edge of the bed as Lenny flopped onto the floor; they were drained.

Jay and Addison waited but were really glad to see Kendal; they weren't so sure about Lenny. After a few minutes of regained strength, Kendal was about to speak but Lenny beat him to it.

"OK, you two keep looking at me. I know. I know. You real surprise to see me. Me too! I real surprise to see me too since your friend here, got us both arrested and then almost killed!" Lenny asserted and carried on as he reached for an uneaten sandwich from the side table. Through chomping he described the events.

"I was just standing there by the station minding my own business, when before I know it Kendal's bitch gets killed!" Lenny declared, as all eyes opened wider in astonishment. He took another bite of the sandwich and carried on while chomping.

"But before he dies, he writes, man, bloody scribbles, one word, one single word. Can you imagine it?" Lenny incredulously asked and carried on.

"Scribbled on a piece of paper." Lenny stated as he stared from Addison to Kendal and then to Jay while at the same time continuing to devour the ham sandwich.

Jay and Addison were doing the same, not eating but staring from Lenny to Kendal as each word sprung out of Lenny's mouth as if it was impatiently thrown by his tongue, so that his stomach could be filled with the food. Jay and Addison could not understand it all but kept silent as Lenny carried on.

"What is it that you all, into? Why you all hold up in this B & B?" Lenny suspiciously asked as he wolfed down and finished the sandwich. Next, he rapidly turned and opened a can of cola which promptly disappeared down his throat.

"Lenny, please go back to what was written on the paper." Kendal requested.

"I didn't see the paper everything happened so fast." Kendal indicated.

Turning away slightly, Lenny reached into his mouth and pulled out a top plate of false teeth. The three watched with complete amazement and revulsion in their eyes.

Lenny then held the teeth in his hand, turned them over and pulled out a piece of paper which was stuck to the inner side of the plate in what looked like a hole. He next held the wet paper in his hand and spoke.

"Lost all my teeth in fights." Lenny remarked and adoringly looked at his false ones before continuing.

"Now don't go getting any ideas that I actually lost them fights. You see, I bite like a tiger!" He bragged and went on.

"These false teeth are one of my winning trophies!" Lenny boasted. He next broadly grinned, which broke into a toothless smile. Jay wondered what other missing body parts did Lenny have, which represented winning fighting awards but she kept quiet.

"Lenny, what is on the paper and how did you get it from the police?" Kendal surprisingly queried.

"These teeth here, work really well. When arrested, the police can't confiscate these teeth. It is against my human rights. Great place for hiding things." Lenny said and once more showed a toothless smile.

"You see, this is the paper Kendal's bitch scrawled the word on, and I pushed it under my false teeth plate, just before they could handcuff me." Lenny bragged.

He glanced at the paper and turned to Kendal.

"Decent pen Kendal, ink still good. The writing is visible." Lenny detailed as he held them all in eager suspense while looking the paper over.

"What is the word which the man wrote?" Kendal impatiently asked.

"Look, see." Lenny said as he pointed the paper in Kendal's direction.

"Tell me." Kendal abruptly said, not wanting to touch the soggy paper. Lenny held up the paper with one hand while fixing his teeth back into his mouth with the other.

"The bitch wrote, steal. You hear. It is marked steal!" Lenny curiously stated and went on.

"What the hell that means? What kinda things you and that skinny China man were going to do? Kendal? Miss Loraine ain't going to be pleased." Lenny warned.

Lenny's remarks made Kendal's skin go all cold. His mother, he thought must be in absolute turmoil with more shock. This would be a big blow to her, of his face being shown on television as a wanted man, suspected of murder. The police, he thought, must have been over to her. This was all so very serious. Abruptly he was now pulled away from his mind-blowing thoughts, as Lenny spoke once more.

"Kendal, you coulda seriously broken some part of that man's body if you laid on him, I bet. He weighed less than powder, in a girl's compact." Lenny joked.

"Lenny, this is extremely grim. I was meeting him just to get some information." Kendal explained and went on."What the hell does steal mean?" Kendal queried as he looked at each one of the three people, hoping to get some kind of insight.

"Don't look at me; he was your bitch, not mine." Lenny retorted.

Kendal then looked more intently at Jay and Addison who were still mystified by it all and tried to get consent from them, to tell Lenny the whole truth about what they were doing. Jay and Addison gave defeated nods of approval.

Kendal next recounted the night's events for Addison and Jay and then he explained to Lenny what their dire predicament was. After a few minutes everyone was up on events and purposes and after a while Lenny spoke.

"Well, I have nothing to lose beside a holiday behind the barbeque grills, so I might as well help you and at the same time possibly clear my good name." Lenny said and smiled once more.

"It is now 1:30 am and still dark so I suggest that we go either at Jian Ling's place or go back and check out that Dragon Tooth Restaurant." Kendal said.

Everyone stared at Kendal in frightened silence about this plan. They all looked at him as though he was mad. Then Lenny spoke up, breaking the wet strained air in the room.

"I know the Dragon Tooth. You eat there, and instead of prawn crackers, you get extra grease and hair." Lenny piped in.

"Man, I hate greasy food and that old man, is supposed to be a bad ass. So, we have to watch out." Lenny warned and continued speaking.

"Maybe we should go to the Ling man's place first. I saw him once or twice before and he didn't look too fierce. Lenny stated and continued.

"He had Wednesday legs, you know, legs so skinny, that you wondered, when they gonna break and now he is dead, so his place might not be too dangerous." Lenny proposed.

"I know what you mean, and possibly we should, so let's think through everything first." Kendal recommended and continued.

"Somebody had to have been watching the man I was to meet and so they now know us, and we don't know who they are, even though it most likely relates to the Dragon Tooth." Kendal supposed.

"Before that bitc-" Lenny was about to say, what Kendal hated but was cut short.

"Lenny, Lenny, for God's sake, just cut that out. Just say kitchen hand, please?" Kendal begged as he looked at Lenny in desperation. Kendal thought that he could not feel any worse even if he was dying. Lenny looked back with sympathetic humour and merely shook his head; then he carried on.

"As I was saying before the captain here, interrupted me, well kitchen hand, and not Kendal's bitch, was killed, did you not feel a big gush of wind and a puff of something, like smoke go pass us and then, the kitchen hand just started to drop. Did you not feel all that Kendal?" Lenny asked.

"Yes. I remember now. I think that it was someone on a bicycle whizzing pass. Then, I managed to hear the coroner say that it looked as though it was poison, from a dart or needle, something like that." Kendal explained.

"Now if that is some kinda shit poison, you know, all them herbal potions and mixtures, that they use on him, in the neck, then we have to be extremely careful, otherwise we could end up like him." Lenny paused and then went on.

"Kendal, you saw, how fast it took that kitchen hand down, dead in seconds." Lenny warned. His eyes flickered around the room as if looking for something. While Lenny was doing this, Jay took the opportunity to speak.

"So, he didn't get a chance to tell you anything at all? She asked.

"Nothing. Except the word on the paper that Lenny has. Steal. I have absolutely no idea what that means." Kendal said.

He was now watching as Lenny dragged a blanket from the cupboard, while Jay continued speaking.

"So, meeting him just got us into more trouble. Not one single lead, to help us find out who killed

Sage." Jay whined. Listening to Jay but watching Lenny caused Kendal to ignore Jay for a minute, and so he did not reply to her, but turned to Lenny.

"Lenny, have you gone more insane?" Kendal asked as he watched in alarm, as Lenny cut the B & B's blanket into long strips. Lenny looked at Kendal and spoke.

"Why don't you answer Mona Lisa first, before paying attention to me?" Lenny asked and continued cutting the blanket.

"Have you forgotten her name? It is Jay, not Mona Lisa." Kendal replied.

"Well, you coulda fool me! All this bloody moaning that Jay doing, she should change her name to Mona Lisa!" Lenny heatedly responded as his intent on cutting increased to feverish pace. Jay just watched and then she spoke.

"We are in a lot of trouble and have no information whatsoever but now we have added to it, with Lenny the loser, who's cutting up property that we will have to pay for." Jay angrily asserted.

Lenny just calmly looked at Jay.

"Jay that is a bit below minimum wage but I don't work for anyone so I will take it like a man and ignore your comment." Lenny said and continued speaking.

"I agreed to help you all but I ain't easily sentencing myself to death." Lenny stated.

"Sorry Lenny." Jay softly apologized.

"I generally forgive posthumously but for you, I make the exception." Lenny smiled at Jay as he continued his cutting.

The three just watched Lenny with open eyes and closed lips. Kendal really did not want quarrelling between them.

"I am cutting up this blanket for a real good reason." Lenny emphatically stated and went on explaining.

"We will each take a piece and wrap it thickly around our necks to stop any poison darts from getting through to our flesh if the killers get to us." Lenny specified.

Straightaway, he demonstrated by first wrapping a long piece of the blanket several times around his neck. They all watched in astonishment.

Consequently, with a mixture of discomposure and uneasiness, like crazed people, they all did the same. Kendal then took a coin out of his pocket and next turned to everyone.

"Enough talking, heads the Dragon Tooth, tails the Jian Ling's place." Kendal said as he tossed the coin into the air.

It rolled, flipped over and settled at Jay's feet. She looked down at it with dread. She was terrified of either side of the coin. She just stared at it as the others waited expectantly on her to stoop and pick it up.

In slow motion she bent with an out stretched hand. No matter which side the coin landed on, Jay knew that great threat and danger would be waiting for them. Her hand trembled and shook as she slowly lifted the coin.

Chapter Fifteen

Tormenting fear and anxiety were equally shared, amongst these four young people, as they set out to Jian Ling's address. The coin had settled it, their destination had been determined. They kept low and were glad that Lenny knew all of the off beaten paths of the city's back streets.

Their hearts were racing. Their legs produced extraordinary sprints every now and then, to run at full throttle over interspersed short distances. They were swiftly propelled along so fast, that their ankles strained under the enormous pressure of never having both feet on the ground at the same time.

The police were everywhere. Sirens took up residence in the dense night air which was filled with smoke from the continuing explosions. Just before they left the B & B, Kendal recalled the news broadcast reported, that the Sainsbury wing of the National Gallery had completely melted and this had caused extensive structural damage to the entire building which was now also on fire. The shockwave of the explosion had killed many, by sucking the air out of the lungs of people in adjacent buildings.

Kendal, Jay, Addison and Lenny, had been on edge as they had waited and listened while the grisly broadcast went from bad to horrendous; the building had also melted. The broadcast went on to say that the London Eye and St Pancras Station had all been totally wiped out, melted. Fatalities and casualties were rising by the minute. Still, no one had claimed responsibility for these attacks and the Cobra Committee was in session. The Police Serious Crime Division was seeking the public's assistance in providing information surrounding the attacks.

Now on the run, and still searching for Sage's killer, Kendal's mind could only fleetingly reflect, that somehow what they were doing seemed inconsequential, compared to all of the upheaval within the city. Still, Sage's life could not be callously thrown into this melting pot of hopelessness and left there. His stomach was a tight rope, twisting in knots and his heart was not beating; it was stamping inside his chest.

As they neared Duck Lane, he was preparing himself for something bad to happen. Shortly, they had entered the lane. The four swiftly hid behind four large garbage bins to survey the area. All eyes were smarting from the smoky city air but they still rapidly danced around, eyeing up this cul de sac. Kendal felt certain that he could hear the loud thumping beats of his own heart and that of the others. He now quietly turned to whisper to his friends.

"There is one police guarding but others could also be watching from another building." Kendal whispered and carried on.

"But probably too busy with all these attacks; I feel that we should chance it. It's now or never." He said, as all heads kept slowly swinging about, looking and keeping on guard.

"OK, see that door to the side, there should be the plant pot which the woman was reaching into from the Google Street view, where I guess a key is." Kendal outlined.

"What if you are wrong and there's no key, uh?" Jay softly asked.

"Too late now, I'll go first to look for the key. If I find it, I will put my hand in my back pocket as the signal for you all to come." Kendal said.

Lenny peered at the door of 8B Duck Lane, as though expecting to see the door pushed opened at any time.

"Hold it Kendal, but who says that, that man lived alone? Maybe, just maybe someone else lives there and is, in there right now." Lenny worriedly pointed out.

"In that dingy little dark place?" Kendal sarcastically asked.

"Well excuse me, but those Chinese are small and little. Man, a lot of them do live under one roof as an extension family." Lenny blurted out.

"Extended, extended family, Lenny." Addison corrected.

"Hey man, this ain't no time for grammar lessons." Lenny hurriedly retorted.

Then he stooped and picked up a black cat that was slinking by and started to stroke it. The others gave him a weird look questioning his affection for a cat at this time.

"We need to first distract that police; it's a woman officer. I am sure that she can see that door." Lenny whispered.

With no further speaking, Lenny crept up behind the tree which was close to the officer and threw the cat onto her shoulders. The cat violently screeched and scratched. The police officer lost her balance and fell over. As the officer and the cat tried to disentangle themselves, Lenny stealthily sprinted back to his surprised team.

"What the hell you waiting for, man? Go! Kendal! We will watch out for you. Go! Go now! Go!" Lenny quickly urged.

In a flash, Kendal scurried the short distance to reach the other side of the lane. He jumped over the small gate and very soon he had his hand in the pot. He felt around in the soil and then his fingers hit on a cold metal object. He pulled it up and thankfully it was indeed a key.

Kendal gratefully breathed out, relieved that his assumptions had been correct and that he had found the key. He then put his hand in his back pocket as the signal for the others to come. Instantly, they all soundlessly bounded across the road and shuffled through the gate. The police officer was still trying to regain composure at the front, as she slowly got up and dusted her uniform off.

In the meantime, Kendal quickly wiped the soil off of the key and pushed it into the keyhole. The door opened and then staring right back at them, was another inner door, with an almighty big lock.

"What the fuck?" Lenny whispered as he peered from behind Kendal.

"Man, what the hell are we going to do?" Addison asked, as Kendal stood still.

"Shift yourself, stone man." Lenny instructed Kendal as he tried to get to the front to reach the door.

Lenny dived into his deep pockets and pulled out what looked like a small flask but it had a concealed inner tube. Inside this tube, Lenny removed what looked like a mini utility set. A small skewer and a tweezers were also pulled out. Lenny pushed the skewer-like implement into the lock and then he twisted and pulled with the tweezers. A small clink was heard and the door slowly opened.

Lenny peeped inside and then one by one they stealthily entered. Darkness blanketed the room. Damp and mould sealed the windows and created choking air which lodged itself in the airways of the four. Although the room was damp it now became uncomfortably warm from the body heat of anxiety of the four. They slackened the thick pieces of blanket which they were wearing as protection around their necks.

The room was so dreadfully small that they almost filled the cramped space. They stepped about gingerly as the floor boards creaked under the pressure of their feet.

Everyone's eyes were searching but it seemed that there was nothing to be seen. All that was there were a small bed, and a freezer, nothing to suggest that this was a business man's home. Kendal searched in this freezer to find out if it had any hidden compartments but if it did, they could see none. Each one stood almost shoulder to shoulder with unease about this uncertain outcome. Then all of a sudden Lenny jumped back, startling the others.

"What's that noise?" He whispered while darting his head in ferret like fashion. They pricked their ears and leaned forward from their edgy queue, to look at Lenny and shake their heads from side to side in voiceless, negative disagreement about the noise.

"Listen. It is a knocking sound." Lenny claimed as he motioned to keep still.

"Quiet. There it is again." He softly insisted.

They all listened once more and very slowly a faint tapping sound was audible.

"Yes. There is a tapping sound." Kendal now softly agreed as he looked around.

"Where's it coming from?" Addison asked.

No one replied. They just listened. Just as Lenny had said, there was a knocking sound but they could not tell where it was coming from. Then muffled cries were also very faintly heard. Lenny bent down and they watched as he put his ear to the floor. He tapped on the boards and waited. In a few seconds a response tap came back. Lenny did this again and the same happened along with muffled indistinct cries as was heard before.

"There is someone under this place." Lenny sharply asserted.

"Wouldn't a basement flat have a concrete floor?" Lenny whispered.

"Yes, but this building is very old so not sure." Kendal replied.

They all felt tense and were afraid of this uncertain noise as Lenny spoke again.

"I don't think that these houses on Duck Lane would have wooden basement floors. So why does this one, have boards?" Lenny suspiciously asked.

Everyone was now on their knees with their ears to the floor, anxiously listening. Their ears were glued to the floor boards. The stillness of the room became eerie and it suddenly started to feel cold once more.

"We have to try to raise this floor board where this noise is coming from." Lenny softly stressed.

Jay tipped toed to the tiny sink and found a knife. Lenny looked up at her.

"You not planning to use that on me?" Lenny jokingly queried.

"Not yet, Lenny. Just see if this will help raise the board." Jay teasingly told him, as she passed the knife.

"There is someone under here. Do you hear the tapping again?" Lenny softly asked, as he started to prise up the board. He stuck the knife into the crease of the board but the knife broke and nothing else moved.

"Bloody hell, cheap knife. The board just ain't moving." Lenny frustratingly said.

"Hear it again? The tapping, who the hell could be under there?" Lenny queried once more. Rapidly using the broken knife, he was losing energy and the board was not shifting. Abruptly stopping, he looked at the others who were bending beside him.

"Man, we will have to go and get a crowbar or something stronger to lift this board because I am sure that somebody is under here." Lenny declared.

"By the time we go back outside it will be light and the sun will be rising soon." Addison worriedly said.

Lots of deep breaths could be heard and then Jay continued.

"We will be clearly seen coming back to this place, why don't we just tell the police outside there, what we think?" Jay worriedly asked.

"Of course. Sure. Yes, we can. With explosions everywhere and Kendal and I are wanted men, we can just expect to be arrested and also blamed for these explosions and murders!" Lenny hotly specified as he glared at Jay.

"We could leave a note or call anonymously." Jay outlined.

"Yes, you think this is a fairy tale story. Tell the police and they all lived happily ever after." Lenny mocked and went on.

"This is a big city, with big ass problems and big suspicions right now. I ain't taking that chance!" Lenny exclaimed a bit too loudly as the tapping below resumed.

"Shush! Shush!" Addison interjected.

"I agree with Lenny. We need to concentrate on what we set out to do and this is part of it." Kendal softly asserted and went on.

"We get a crowbar and take up this board, something is going on here and this after all, is where Jian Ling lived or so we believe." Kendal explained.

They all looked at Kendal but he could not determine Addison and Jay's feelings since they both had empty stares. Lenny then put his ear to the floor once more and then commented.

"I bet that, that man you all worked for, that Jian man, is into some kind a kinky shit." Lenny stated and carried on.

"You all worked for him as the phantom customers and clients, who write them blogs and reviews for numerous companies, yeah?" Lenny commented and carried on as he resumed pulling at the floor board.

"Them companies paid him to get their goods and services selling fast." Lenny said as he took a few more digs at the board and also at his friends.

"In your reviews and blogs, you praise, approve and big up, their products and services, which you have never seen, bought or used." Lenny paused as if pondering on that thought and then he went on speaking.

"Your feedback on the item or service is so excellent, that it is soaked up by the masses and spurs them on to happily part with their money, yeah?" Lenny remarked as he pulled a splinter from his finger nail.

"All based on your ratings and reviews. Lots of smart consumer manipulation." Lenny accused as he looked up at the three, who were standing and watching him.

"Now, could it be possible, that one really pissed off consumer, had it in for your company man Jian?" Lenny concluded.

They all waited in cold silence, no one spoke. Lenny then stood up in the small and confined space, he could hardly turn but next looked from Kendal to Jay and finally at Addison.

The room was soundless, as the three, held their heads low. Kendal felt that Lenny seemed to be great at putting nails in your coffin and brilliant at the game, of hit a man when he is down. His aim right now was spot on. Lenny then quietly walked, opened the door, peeped outside and they all made a hasty exit sprint, from Duck Lane.

Chapter Sixteen

Between running and walking Lenny led the three to Leicester Square as they dodged every conceivable police officer. In between running and walking, at one stage in time, they felt sure that a hooded man on a motor bike had been shadowing them and were glad for wearing the protective pieces of blanket around their necks. In efforts to escape this possible deadly foe, they increased their speedy momentum, by following Lenny through small back street shops and existing on alley ways, which they never knew existed, but aided them in losing their ominous tail.

They finally applied foot brakes outside of Big Red Safe Storage Unit. They were tired and exhausted and glad that this marathon of physical and mental exertion had now subsided for the time being at least. They leaned back against the cold wall, panting and waited as Lenny tapped in the number codes on the door's security keypad lock.

Within a few seconds, they were inside what appeared to be Lenny's treasure trove; a store of valuable and delightful things. What every criminal's dream is made of, was cast right before their eyes.

Kendal, Jay and Addison stood back as Lenny instructed them not to touch anything. Kendal thought that it was great advice since he did not want to leave their finger prints behind, on any of this highly prison-attracting merchandise. Lenny went further into his cavernous den and emerged with arms laden.

"One for each of us, here you go, here you go, and here you go." Lenny offered as he chucked things at them one by one.

"What's all this? I thought we only came for a crowbar." Kendal stated.

"Bro, can you not see all that is happening out there? Buildings melting, big time panic and of course us. Two wanted men." Lenny stated, as he had shoved reflective yellow police jackets at each one of them, along with police hats.

Kendal, Jay and Addison had no choice but to take the police gear from Lenny. They held the police jackets in their hands and just stared at them. Lenny looked at the three and then he irritably spoke.

"Man, what the hell are you waiting for? Christmas? It's coming! But bloody well not right now! In December!" Lenny impatiently shouted as he hurriedly put his police jacket on.

Kendal, Jay and Addison slowly followed Lenny's lead and dressed themselves in the highly visible yellow jackets and hats. They watched Lenny as he spoke once more.

"We have to blend in. We can't call attention to ourselves." Lenny said and continued.

"What's the best way to blend in at this crazy time but to become part of the police force?" Lenny smirked.

He then passed out several bottles of energy drinks and they all nicely quenched their parched throats. From his repertoire of illegal preparedness, Lenny next passed out tools which they all stuffed into their jacket pockets. After this, Lenny impatiently shuffled them out into the cold air and relocked his business premises. They set out to retrace their steps back to Duck Lane. They hurriedly walked along in pairs but this city scene was far from the usual; it was filled with anguish and despair.

As they turned on to Shaftesbury Ave, their steps quickened. Jay and Addison were walking to the front, while Kendal and Lenny held up the rear. Kendal and Lenny both looked back and they could see blaring lights approaching.

A police vehicle was careening in their direction. The engine noise was deafening. Impact was imminent. Lenny and Kendal instantly grabbed the shoulders of Jay and Addison and jumped with them further onto the pavement. The car sharply zigzagged, barely missing them.

The four lay mangled and intertwined but were instantly struggling to stand as the most tremendous explosion was next heard, followed by fragments of debris hitting them in their faces and dust showering them from head to toe!

In a little while they managed to stand and when they looked towards where the vehicle went, they noticed that it had completely melted.

Loud voices next followed and resounded. The shouts were ringing through the air and stinging their ears. The yelling and the cries were head-splitting as numerous people approached them.

"Officers! Officers! The Shaftesbury Theatre is on fire! It is burning! The Shaftesbury's melting!" The voices were from screaming people as they ran past in fear. Just then, another police vehicle pulled up in front of the disconcerted four. They watched in slow horror as the door of the police transit van was thrown wide open and orders rushed right out from the passenger side of the van as a police sergeant leaned out.

"Get in! Get in! We need more assistance on Regent Street. Get in!" The sergeant bellowed.

Running away was not an option and so they held their heads low and quickly crawled into the van.

"Every store on Regent Street is on fire. You must have heard on your radios." The sergeant informed.

"Our radios just knocked out of our hands back by the Shaftesbury fire." Lenny promptly replied.

Anxiety and panic were gripping the four as they watched the sergeant who started searching into the supply box while his partner steered the car with speedy precision.

"Who is your Division Inspector?" The police sergeant queried.

Lenny looked at Kendal and in a flash Kendal responded.

"Detective Inspector Landry." Kendal mumbled. Thankfully his brain had not deserted him like his courage had. He was really glad that he had recalled the name of the police officer who had interviewed them in the mobile police unit when All Wired Up was on fire. The sergeant next pulled out something from the box he was rummaging in and shoved it in Lenny's direction.

"Here take this and put in your code, only got one." The sergeant said as he gave Lenny a police communication radio. Lenny fumbled around pretending that he was punching keys as he talked to divert and get attention away from them.

"Nasty, awful, business, all this, isn't it?" Lenny declared.

"We have our hands full. Every part of the city is being hit and yet this started on Friday night and it is now early Sunday morning and no one has yet claimed any responsibility." The sergeant regretted.

"If they did, then we would have a focus to target but this anonymous state is horrible to be in." He moaned.

"Strange that, this could be a single person with a big grudge, maybe he or she had a really bad fish and chips meal. Really greasy and now hates the city of London." Lenny joked.

The sergeant shook his head and spoke with Lenny while the three were overflowing with panic at being found out.

"We have to end this and fast." The sergeant asserted and smiled at Lenny's quip.

"Oh, this is some serious shi-"Lenny broke off as he swiftly caught himself and quickly switched to a better selection of words.

"We are the Metropolitan Police and nothing can defeat us." Lenny added and gave a broad smile to the sergeant.

Kendal, Addison, and Jay all felt hot and cold all at the same time, especially cold in places where they should have been warm. The three felt for sure, that they had wet themselves with abject fright. All

Kendal could think was, how the hell would they get out of this?

Chapter Seventeen

Without further delay, Kendal and his friends ran as fast as they could after being dropped off from the police vehicle on Regent Street. They had mingled with the other officers and then had made their speedy departure amidst the fiery commotion. In time, they had finally made it back to Jian's place, thankfully eluding their shadowy motor cyclist tail.

Once more, they evaded the on-guard police's detection. Kendal approached the door and retrieved the key from his pocket that he had carried with him as his friends closely followed. They easily entered the second door since they had not locked it back on leaving.

Right away, Kendal tapped the floor and waited but this time there was no response tapping. He looked at Lenny and Addison and the three went to work on lifting the floor boards while Jay kept a close look out from the tiny window.

After a while they managed to lift the boards but to their dismay, they could feel the concrete coming at them, the brick wall experience! There was nothing.

Lenny and Addison remained slumped over the floor but Kendal started to pace in bewildered anger. They could not see anything besides the cement which was under the flooring boards.

"No, we can't be wrong. There was tapping coming from under there. We just can't be wrong." He angrily cried.

Lenny stood up and started wildly looking all around and then he spoke.

"This is why I could never be a policeman. I can't handle this being stumped thing." Lenny remarked and went on.

"Now what is inside this place that we have not really seen? There has to be some clue in here, something that does not belong." Lenny reasoned.

"Yeah, right Lenny. This ain't that kids' song." Jay chided and continued.

"One of these things is not like the other." Jay irritatingly sang.

Lenny breathed out and then gave as good as he got.

"I ain't even going to answer that, Jay. You are a real misery guts. Probably think you are a carrot and now want everybody to be the mud so you can plant yourself nicely, to grow in?" Lenny crossly responded.

Instantly, Jay jumped up and angrily flew at Lenny. Kendal and Addison had to get in between them to prevent serious muscle carnage from occurring. After a short while of wrestling to keep Jay away from Lenny, Addison now settled her back at the window while Kendal stood in front of Lenny, who talked over Kendal's shoulder, inciting more wrath from Jay.

Neither Kendal nor Addison wanted to deal with this, at this time. They tried as best as they could to diffuse the Jay and Lenny hostility bomb. Finally, Lenny's last address to Jay came and everyone was hoping that the feuding would stop and that they could concentrate before the police heard them.

"Just keep peeping out that window with your mouth closed." Lenny ordered as Jay looked at him with evil eyes but remained silent.

Now turning his attention to Kendal and at the same time looking around the room, Lenny resumed his analysis of the room contents.

"You said that you looked in the back of that Dragon Tooth restaurant and that there was a strange freezer." Lenny intently said, as he walked over to the freezer which was squeezed tightly onto the bed.

"Now this room ain't got much space so why have an empty freezer? Not even a fridge but a freezer?" Lenny probed as he examined the appliance.

"Smack bang in a tiny place like this." He delved deeper.

Lenny's trend of thought was arousing rapid interest. Kendal and Addison drew closer and they both looked inside the freezer again; it was empty and had no hidden compartment. Then Lenny pushed the freezer more to one side, and Kendal pushed his hand, all along the outside of it. Soon, his hand hit on a huge screw that seemed to be holding the side together; he yanked it. Before their eyes the small bed slid and an opening appeared in the floor. They stared in total surprise and shock, down through a big gaping hole with tiny steps!

"Holy shit!" Lenny cried and jumped back.

"Shush, Shush. Don't know who can hear us down there." Kendal whispered.

"Let's see precisely what's down here. Shall we?" Kendal apprehensively asked.

Without replying, one by one they lowered themselves through the floor's opening. They used the torches which Lenny had equipped them with, light spotting intermittently, as their bodies shook in the mysterious dark descent.

"Do you see that, Kendal? What kinda sick shit is that?" Lenny asked as he looked upwards and pulled on a hook which revealed another concealed space.

Glancing up as they went, they could see what looked like a hammock suspended from directly underneath the room which they had just left.

"Wow man! Can you also see the dangling handcuffs?" Kendal queried.

"Man, your boss, that Jian man, I told you, must have some weird, sick fetish. That tapping must have come from one of his sick bondage games." Lenny speculated.

They continued the climb down, to what appeared to be never ending steep steps. It was as though they were entering the bowels of the city. In a short while, the whiffs which they were getting as they made their descent, were now distinctly revealed to them. They were in the city's sewer!

Facing them now were two paths; they had to choose either travelling to the left or to the right. They all looked at Lenny for wisdom in this option.

"Hey man! Don't look at me. I ain't no sewer rat!" Lenny angrily declared.

"Calm down Lenny, just thought that you might know-" Kendal was cut short.

"Just thought that I might know shit! Well, hell no!" Lenny heatedly replied and stared at them with a riled countenance before calmly speaking once more.

"Well, if it wasn't for bad luck, I wouldn't have any luck at all. I guess this is why I always get all of these shit jobs." Lenny rabbited on as they all stared dependently at him.

"Well, we might as well go to the right and we will reach Soho. The left will take us to Fareham Street where you lot used to work. This must have been a real inspiring and enlightening short cut to work, for your sicko boss." Lenny sneered.

The three watched him and marveled at his underground city knowledge. Kendal quickly ran what Lenny said through his mind and if Jian was into no good, then it was highly probable that Lenny was right. This could have been his route, but to where? Kendal wondered.

Lenny started walking and right away they followed him all the while gingerly stepping in, increasingly deeper puddles of filthy water. All kinds of soiled matter were attaching to their trousers and reflective police jackets.

Soon they couldn't decide which was worse, the acrid stench or the rising deluge of untreated sewage which they found themselves floating in. Both were equally vile!

Even though neither choice was good, it seemed that there was not much better above ground because every so often loud explosive bangs could be heard as an indication that the city was still under attack. Lenny also was tuned into his new possession of the police radio, which kept them up to speed on the distressing events.

Additionally, not too deep in Kendal's mind, was the single word which the dying kitchen hand had scribbled across the piece of paper. That solitary word steal, he just could not understand what was significant about it. Suddenly, it was pushed from his thoughts. Lenny's voice could be heard silencing them. They stopped as he paused. He looked at them and then whispered.

"I think that we are under the Dragon Tooth." Lenny believed.

"How do you know? Are you sure?" Kendal asked.

"Can you not feel the denseness and smell of this stinking water?" Lenny asked as he rubbed his fingers together.

"All of the water is messy from right up at the top where we first started from." Kendal softly reminded Lenny.

"Well can't you all not smell and feel grease, like it going out a style? Tons of it and if you can't recognize it, as the signature dish of the Dragon

Tooth, then your senses definitely want realigning." Lenny asserted and carried on looking around.

"Quick! Look to your left." Lenny urged everyone.

"It looks like a trap door." Addison observed.

"Yeah, it is a door of some kind." Jay confirmed as she swung her head around. Lenny's voice softly resounded again.

"Worse. Don't look up at the tiny black hole on its top. I bet that, that is a concealed camera." Lenny described and quickly continued.

"Quick! Keep your faces, down, don't look up." Lenny anxiously whispered.

"What shall we do?" Addison asked as Jay held on to his jacket. He could sense that she was about to panic and he really did not know what to do. He looked at Kendal and Lenny. They just looked right back with absolute discomfort.

"Just keep cool. Wearing these police clothes might keep them off if they saw us already." Kendal reasoned.

"They had to have made us; somebody has to be monitoring that camera." Lenny assumed and carried on.

"Move very slowly up to the side of the trap door. Keep faces down and then we can see if we can open it." Lenny instructed.

Kendal knew that he was at a sure quarter past three on the clock face of disturbing fear. Addison, he felt, was further on, at around a five thirty position. Looking at Jay, he was certain that the lowest on the clock was six thirty but Jays' face showed that all the hands of the clock of abject fear had fallen off! She was in complete distress but neither he nor Addison was very far off from Jay's clock!

Kendal now tried desperately to concentrate more as they paddled in the excrement saturated waters. It was a great effort to resist urging and being sick. Kendal was grateful that they had not really eaten anything, since even to eject matter from the stomach through the mouth, would have been a death-wish inducing occurrence!

As these thoughts filtered through his upset mind, like a shot, a flap which they had not seen suddenly dropped down, beside their heads. The bearded old man appeared. He was lying on his stomach aiming a gun at them. Jay turned to wade away as Addison held her hand but instantly a shot ran out with deafening resonance. The two instantly froze.

"Don run! Stop or I shoot!" The bearded old man thundered as a rope ladder was thrown down through the hole.

"Girl first! If any a you run, girl get shot. Come! come!" He ordered Jay.

Jay had no choice; she trembled as the bearded old man hoisted her up and pushed her straight into the arms of the chef who gripped her tightly. Kendal, Lenny and Addison were powerless to try anything.

"You! You! And then you, up, up! It any a you run, girl, and next one get shot!" The bearded old man menacingly declared.

Their legs wobbled as their brains tried to process these deadly orders. They had no choice but to follow these ghastly instructions. As they climbed up, Kendal could not believe, that they were a full, three hundred and sixty degrees back where they had started out from! This was a terrifying experience. It was Déjà vu at its worst!

Chapter Eighteen

In the meantime, the phone buzzed to wake Landry and Riley. The alarm was persistent until Riley finally stopped it. They had gone off duty to get a few hours of rest. Just in the back of their office, on two sofas they had stretched as best as they could to try to sleep but it was a veritable enemy that only arrived a few minutes ago and now it was time to start their shift once more.

The two detectives took turns in the wash room to attend to personal care. Following this, they promptly went to a 7 am Cobra Defense Committee meeting with a Military General, the Commissioner of Police, Special Forces Inspectors and Fire Chiefs. Environmental Scientists were also present.

They took their coats and it was evident that the room was filled with a variety of subdued thoughts and mixed ideas which all had to be sorted and clearly understood if they were to bring this terror to a halt.

The Commissioner of Police had the first right to speak. He was tall and his uniform and stature was imposing and demanded respect and attention in these troubled times. He looked through his spectacles and then spoke.

"It is now over twenty-four hours since the start of this explosive decay of our city. It commenced with two murders and one building but has now escalated to a near catastrophe, unprecedented human injury and death has resulted. This is a colossal aberration." The Commissioner paused and looked around the room; his eyes striking everyone.

Riley felt that this was no time for speeches but rather they should be getting on with finding those responsible. None the less, he sat tight and listened, as each head of security or emergency service, expounded their views on what was happening in the city.

"No one has yet claimed responsibility for any of these atrocities. So, what can we make of it? Or how can we know who or which building is next?" The General asked.

The Commissioner of Police shot his eyes directly to Riley and Landry. The two inspectors sat up.

"Riley and Landry do you have any leads whatsoever?" The Commissioner of Police asked.

"We are not at all sure that this is terrorist linked. It has the face of something else which we are trying to figure out." Riley informed.

"Please tell us what face that maybe." The Commissioner of Police probed.

"Well for instance, last night a young man was murdered near Piccadilly Station. He has been identified as Kyong Rang. On investigation he travelled here from South Korea, having made it there, from North Korea." Riley paused before going on.

He looked at his captive audience who was now highly visually connected to him. Riley looked at them and then carried on.

"He was killed using a chemical which is prevalent in North Korea and used there for euthanasia. It was inflicted through a dart to the neck." Riley explained.

The leaders around the table all sat up as though they were pricked from behind with a sharp object. Riley could feel their eyes on his lips catching every word which he uttered. He continued.

"The two people found at the murder scene and who were subsequently arrested, albeit escaped, most likely have some kind of information." Riley stated and continued.

"Landry and I have to find evidence to really fit them into this murder scene and these explosions." Riley outlined. He then handed over the floor to Landry.

"We are working on the theory that the two men under suspicion for the murder, could have been paid to carry out the murder of the young North Korean." Landry detailed and paused before continuing.

"We think that this North Korean man, Kyong Rang, had some kind of connection to something or someone criminal and so he had to be silenced." Landry explained and went on.

"Riley and I believe that the first fire at All Wired Up, is somehow connected to these other explosive acts but we don't know how as yet." Landry described as he continued outlining their investigations.

"One of the men at the murder scene last night, and who was charged under suspicion of murder for this North Korean, was indeed an employee of All Wired Up." Landry pointed out and went on speaking.

"We are searching for the owner of the All Wired Up Company since the male corpse from the fire has been now identified and it was not him. Jian Ling is an impostor, with that assumed name, so he is at the top of our list of suspects." Landry detailed.

"What other information do you have on the murdered young North Korean, man?" The Commissioner of Police asked as he surveyed faces.

"We know that he worked as kitchen help at a restaurant on Dean Street called, the Dragon Tooth. He spent most of his time there." Riley stated as his audience were still held by the ears and eyes at the mention of North Korea.

"In a short while we will be going over there to speak with the owner." Riley detailed and continued.

"A search of the young man's bedsit revealed very little. Just like the search of the Jian Ling's place, nothing." Riley informed.

"Whatever reason, that North Korean, Kyong Rang, was killed, probably lies at his work place." Riley concluded.

"I think it best, that you get a warrant to search the Dragon Tooth when you go there. Who is the owner?" The Commissioner inquired.

"A seventy-six-year-old man, originally from Shanghai, called Gang Fan. I should like to point out that his name means powerful and lethal." Riley smirked; Landry knew that Riley had a thing about names.

"His name may very well not be a coincidence in these deadly cases." Landry pointed out and handed the floor over to the Environmental Scientist.

"We have been examining what's left of the buildings and have been assessing the grade of the construction materials used. They all meet the BSI and ISO Standards and so even in the event of fire, these buildings should not melt." The Scientist outlined.

Faces around the table looked baffled and reverted to a state of bleak anticipation, as they continued to listen.

"We are digging into the type of explosive material which is being used but we have not found anything as yet which could produce such superior and advance detonation, leading to complete melt down of structurally sound buildings." The Scientist specified.

He looked around the table and eyes were faltering. He felt that they were all hoping that Science could pinpoint the device or material that was the cause for this disintegration of building matter, which could lead to a place of origin but right now all that the Scientist had, was empty and inconclusive lab results. Disappointment was clearly evident in the room.

"I want to also inform you that there have been numerous reports of people returning containers and bags of molten pots and pans to stores." The Scientist added.

"Are these proven to be actual kitchen utensils? Or are these people trying it on and somehow collecting molten matter from around crime sites?" The Commissioner asked.

"We were sent some of the material from three of the stores and we could not prove or disprove the authenticity of the claims." The Scientist indicated.

"This is extremely puzzling and even more so since no one has claimed responsibility for any of these attacks." The General said.

Just then the meeting was interrupted as an officer knocked on the door. Each person looked at the closed door somewhat irritably at this interruption.

"Isn't there a sign outside that door which says meeting in progress?" The Commissioner frowned as he queried.

"Come." He curtly said.

In walked a sergeant with an anxious look on his face. He stood and nervously waited as the Commissioner looked at him with anticipation.

"Yes? What is it?" The Commissioner brusquely asked.

"Sir, I regret to inform you that we have just received reports that, HMS Defender, HMS Daring, HMS Dauntless, HMS Diamond, HMS Dragon…" The officer's voice faltered and wobbled as he continued reading out the long list of all of the British active Royal Navy ships.

When the officer came to the end of the list of country's defense war ships, he took deep breaths and then he spoke for a second time.

"Sir, I must also inform you that they all have exploded and subsequently melted." The officer gloomily informed as everyone seemed to have turned to stone.

Subsequently, in a flash of words the questions flew at the still and flustered sergeant.

"How? When...?" a continuous flurry of questions was hurled at the officer from all around the room.

"Hum, hum." The officer cleared his throat and the buzz in the room stopped. He looked at the group and continued.

"Sir, I must also inform you that our Military aircraft, AgustaWestland, Beechcraft Avenger, British Aerospace Hawk, Merlin, Lockheed Martin, Westland Sea King..." The officer continued reading out the entire list. Then, he stopped as his voice shook along with his hands that held the iPad which he was reading from. He looked at everyone once more and then continued.

"Sir, I must also immediately notify you that all of our fighter jets, all the landing gear has been destroyed." As these dire words were dropped from the officer's lips so did the iPad which he read from. It tumbled from his hands onto the floor.

Landry and Riley looked around the room, they wondered if this falling list of doom, was symbolic of how now, not only the city but that the entire country was besieged by an unknown force.

Could the failure to prevent this, was now displaying the limits of British power? All eyes hit the officer with hastened and overwhelming alarm, counter action had to be immediate.

Chapter Nineteen

Sunday's sun managed to hold its place in the cloud laden sky. The rays struggled through the thick clouds and a few were now peeping through the slits in the bedroom window blinds. Having gone to bed early on Saturday night, Lorraine now awoke out of what was a very a fitful sleep.

Her mind was still filled with the immediate worry about the murder of Sage and her boss; coupled with this, all of the recent attacks in the city. She now climbed out of bed and headed to the shower. As she was about to undress, her phone rang and she went to the corner of the door and called out.

"Kendal! Kendal! Will you please get that?" Lorraine asked. Not getting any reply, she briskly walked back from the bathroom and picked up the telephone.

"Hello, good morning." Lorraine greeted the caller as the rapidly speaking voice hit her ears.

"What? What? Kendal went out with Jay and Addison and I am sure that I heard him come in last night. What?" Lorraine said.

She was listening to the person at the other end as she walked with the phone. She knocked on Kendal's bed room door but stopped as the caller gave more instructions diverting her to the TV instead.

Lorraine stopped knocking and went downstairs to the TV. Soon standing in front of the TV, Lorraine continued speaking as she reached and switched it on.

"OK I am there now, which channel?" She asked the caller. With the remote in her hand, she tapped in the BBC channel 101. Lorraine's eyes winged onto the TV screen and became stuck like wet paper to a ceiling. She could not unhinge her eyes neither her brain.

"My God! That is my son! Kendal! Kendal? Kendal? Wanted on suspicion of murder? My God!" Lorraine shouted into the phone as she fainted.

"Lorraine? Lorraine? Are you alright? Lorraine? Lorraine!" The frantic voice at the other end of the line shouted into the phone.

No answer came as Lorraine was sprawled across her sitting room carpet with the TV remote and the phone lying beside her. The voice on the other end of the phone continued speaking in alarm at the lack of response from Lorraine.

"I will call an ambulance for you. Lorraine? Lorraine? I will be right over." Sage's mother, Dianne spoke these consoling words into the phone but Lorraine was unable to respond. Dianne then hastily got ready to head over to Loraine's house.

On reflection, Dianne thought that she should not have delivered the news to Lorraine in the way that she did but she too, was in a state of shock when she saw Kendal's face being shown in connection with murder. This was becoming all too much to bear, Dianne thought, as she kissed her grandchildren and hurriedly left the house.

After a while, Lorraine slowly regained consciousness. She looked up and saw the green uniforms of the paramedics and the familiar face of Dianne.

"Lorraine, can you tell me how many fingers I am holding up?" The paramedic asked.

"I need my glasses." Lorraine said as everyone smiled at her being alert. She then sat up and shook her head as she took her spectacles from Dianne and spoke.

"I cannot believe how Kendal could be on the run accused of murder." Lorraine lamented as she tightly held her stomach.

"Let us check your blood pressure and ensure that you have indeed recovered." The paramedic requested.

Lorraine sat back and was thoroughly checked over. She was found to be physically fine even if not emotionally so. She sat silently as a cup of tea was brought to her and she took some sips but then broke into floods of tears.

She then took up a picture frame from the side table. She tightly held the picture of her son in her hand and looked at it with uninterrupted stares until the sound of the doorbell broke her away from her thoughts.

"There's the doorbell, I'll just get it." Dianne said as she walked to the door.

"Good morning." Dianne sadly greeted the police officers as she let them in.

Lorraine met the officers with tears in her eyes. Dianne had the same, two mothers grieving for their children.

"We can get you some support if you wish." The paramedic offered Lorraine and the police agreed before commencing their interrogation. Lorraine looked at them in absolute shock and anguish.

"All I want is my son, the real Kendal to be freed of this charge!" She wailed and continued.

"This day, this very day, in this city of London, is one that I prayed each and every night, to never come to pass!" Lorraine cried and went on speaking.

"That, my son, Kendal, would never, ever, be in any trouble with the police or to have ever done, anyone, any harm whatsoever!" Lorraine wept.

She held her stomach, encircled herself and subsequently concluded.

"My Kendal, my Kendal! He would never do these things but I know that there is no justice in this world!" Lorraine wept.

She and Dianne then burst into floods of tears; two mothers in anguish for two very painful reasons.

Chapter Twenty

Within the confines of Scotland Yard, Landry and Riley were preparing a tactical team to go to the Dragon Tooth Restaurant but were still evaluating and assessing information. They had worked out from updated reports, from the Environmental Scientists, that the people who had brought in melted kitchen appliances were indeed truthful about their accounts. Landry and Riley looked at each other and Riley next spoke.

"What is puzzling me, is why hit the random households and destroy innocuous items and how? Why were these destroyed and not the entire house?" Riley queried.

"I am also really baffled by all of this but there is something else in my head." Landry declared.

"What's that?" Riley asked as he scrutinized more information from the files.

"It is about that, All Wired Up, case. With only one entrance, how is it that in that CCTV footage that we never saw that Parker man entering? How did he get in there?" Landry asked.

"Well, we can't find that out now from the building. All Wired Up is now all burnt up." Riley contributed to the mystery misery.

"All these attacks all started after that All Wired Up building burnt and then melted." Landry pointed out and carried on.

"We have to look at the architectural drawings of that All Wired Up building. Something is a foot with that." Landry speculated as he picked up the phone and called the sergeant.

"Grimes, please get me the architectural drawings for the All Wired Up building." Landry requested and went on.

"I have a hunch, please come into my office." Landry said as he mused over the information once more.

Grimes soon entered the office and speedily sat at the desk computer.

"This shouldn't be too difficult. It is a new build and therefore the plans should be easily accessible. Let me run it through now." Grimes explained.

A few minutes of tapping and Grimes had the plans on the screen. Landry and Riley looked over his shoulder.

"Only one way into that building and one way out." Grimes stated and continued.

"None of the CCTV footage shows Parker entering that building and these plans show no other way in." Grimes reiterated.

The three looked at each other and the jigsaw was growing larger. The three officers stared at the building plans with more questions than answers.

"So how did Parker enter and why, possibly from one of these adjacent buildings?" Landry wearily speculated.

"These drawings do not reveal much at all for any other entrances." Grimes admitted.

Almost sighing, Landry next spoke. "Rest that for a while and we will come back to it. Thanks Grimes." Landry said. Grimes then left their office.

Shifting their attention, reports were rolling in like wild fire that most military equipment, tanks and armored vehicles had all been hit. They had been informed that the Cobra Committee had now raised the threat level to severe. The two detectives now waited to hear what the Honourable Prime Minister was going to say in the address to the nation. They joined the other officers who were present around the TV as the volume was raised. They watched as the Prime Minister spoke.

"I wish to offer my deepest sympathy to those who have experienced personal loss from these tragic and cowardly attacks. Our attackers to date, have not come forward to identify themselves and this can only be construed, that despite the atrocities leveled against us, that we are still seen as a country standing united and as a force which will not be conquered." The Prime Minster paused and then continued.

"I wish to affirm that this unjustified aggression will not topple us from our strength and determination. We will stand together and prevail against this unconscionable and abhorrent hostility. However, it is with much regret that I must announce that the country is now under a state of emergency..." The Prime Minister continued to address the nation.

Landry, Riley and the other officers kept focused on the broadcast. It was now being finally summed up. They listened as the Prime Minister's final view of hope and defense was given.

"I am totally confident that every person within our nation will willingly give their support in these perilous times to prevent this threat to life and freedom from becoming even more disastrous." The Prime Minister concluded the address.

All the police officers returned to their respective desks. Landry and Riley retreated to their office and as they were logging off of their computers, the phone rang. Landry reached across his desk and lifted the phone off its charger.

"Landry speaking, go ahead. That's a surprise." He told the caller and continued.

"This definitely changes some of our thinking on this All Wired Up case. Thanks." Landry informed the caller and replaced the phone. Riley watched and waited for information as related to the call.

"What was that all about? Riley asked the pensive Landry.

"That was the coroner. He just reported on the outcome of the identification process of the second body pulled from All Wired Up fire." Landry slowly relayed this information, as Riley anxiously listened.

"Landry, I get it; it's your turn to keep me in suspense but will you stop fucking about and tell me the full update!" Riley impatiently demanded as he was still awaiting Landry's reply.

Breathing out heavily as if held under a massive object Landry finally spoke.

"This is not messing about, that second body from the All Wired Up fire, has been identified as that of Mae Young; the wife, not cousin, of Parker Davies." Landry informed and went on speaking.

"This not only changes things but muddles them even more. So where is Sage Murphy? And how are all of these young people involved in these attacks?" Landry's baffled question rang out.

Before the two men could collect their thoughts on this new piece of information, just then sergeant Grimes knocked on the door and he was asked to enter. Landry and Riley waited to hear what update he had.

"Riley and Landry we just had a call from sergeant Moorcroft." Grimes stated.

"Yes? And what it is in relation to?" Landry inquired as he stared at Grimes.

"Sergeant Moorcroft has asked if your four officers have been safely accounted for since this early morning fires on Regent Street." Grimes explained.

"We did not have any officers on Regent Street they were busy elsewhere." Riley outlined.

"Sergeant Moorcroft has also said that he lent a radio to one of the four police officers who said that Landry was their Division Inspector." Grimes explained and carried on.

"The radio should have been coded and returned but it has not been." Grimes detailed.

"Could Moorcroft have gotten the name of the Division Inspector wrong? And could these officers have been hurt?" Landry queried as he looked at Riley who appeared very pensive.

"Hum, very strange. No one has been unaccounted for. Tell sergeant Moorcroft that we will find who has the radio and where it presently is." Landry informed and went on.

"Grimes, put an immediate location trace on that radio and keep us informed of its position." Landry instructed.

"Everything has to be suspected at this time no matter how small or insignificant it may seem to be." Riley asserted.

"On it! Sir." Grimes assured as he left the room.

"Now let's get the team ready for the Dragon Tooth. I am not liking that North Korean link at all." Riley uncomfortably declared.

Chapter Twenty-One

Trapped with no way out, Kendal, Lenny, Addison and Jay were captives held under the Dragon Tooth. All Kendal could recall was that a dirty rag had been placed across their faces as soon as they had climbed to the top of the ladder. Unlike its grimy looks, it had a pleasant-smelling and colourless liquid on it. Waking now groggy, and disoriented, this rag he now realized, had to have been laced with Ether and some other potent drug.

Looking around he could see that they had been placed in small individual cages, the type used to confine animals. The four were stripped to the waist, wearing only under garments and their clothes taken. They were cold and shivering as fear and hunger had drained the energy from their bodies.

In the blackness, Kendal could still see that there was no door. There were no sounds apart from a resonating continuous buzzing and the blackness though intense, was broken by tiny streams of artificial light.

Kendal looked at their cages and he could see each of his friends slowly coming around but everyone's hands were handcuffed behind their backs, except Jay's.

Jay's breathing was unsteady as she rolled and hit the sides of her enclosure like a sick hamster with no escape. Her eyes slowly opened and she quickly covered her breasts.

Lenny was now fully conscious, aware of, and responding to his surroundings; his confinement in a cage. Lenny was a wild parrot as he furiously screamed, at being caged.

"Let me the fuck out!" Lenny shrieked in such a high-pitched piercing sound that Kendal feared that they would be shot.

"Shush! Shush!" Kendal softly called out as Lenny's shrieking now fully raised Addison from his drugged stupor as he opened his swollen eye lids.

Kendal watched, and liked a caged angry bird, Lenny violently fluttered and moved in all directions by turning the cage over and over until it rested in front of Jay's cage. Lenny raised his head to Jay but she looked away. He rolled himself closer but Jay held her hands tighter to her chest.

"Move you pervert." Jay screamed.

"Look Jay, do I look like I want to get it on? Or do I look like I want to get us all out of these fucking cages?" Lenny yelled.

"You are a pissing moron! Get away from me." Jay screeched.

"Lenny! Lenny! What is it that you want from Jay?" Kendal demanded as he acted as an intermediary between these two caged enemies.

"What it is I want? I want her to try to fucking help me to get us out of these cages!" Lenny yelled and carried on.

"Her hands are free. I have a pin under my false teeth but my hands and everybody else's are tied except Jay's." Lenny stressed and carried on.

"All Miss asshole has to do is take out my teeth and get the pin and pick the bloody lock on the cage! Then I can free you all. Plain and simple!" Lenny heatedly outlined.

"You pissing mad if you really think that I will put my hand in your mouth! I rather kiss a bear!" Jay bellowed.

"Shush! Shush! Please Jay." Kendal begged.

"Well, if you don't do it, we all will be kissing them fucking dragons that locked us up, not your bear!" Lenny angrily warned.

"Jay, Jay!" Kendal called out once more but Jay refused to answer. Addison now became more alert and rolled his cage nearer to Jay's and Lenny's.

Kendal watched and hoped that Addison could convince Jay to help.

"Jay, Jay! Come on please do as Lenny is asking. Remember back in the B & B?" Addison coaxed.

Jay shifted her feet. This was hopefully an indication that she would respond to Lenny. Addison continued.

"We promised each other that if we got out of this, that we would start a life together." Addison continued.

"I love you and you love me but we can't have a life together if we don't get out of this." Addison lovingly cajoled.

"Jay all of this love can flow later between you and Addison if you just please, for the love of God, take out my teeth!" Lenny pleaded.

Lenny, Kendal and Addison all watched Jay. At that point they felt that she would never do as Lenny had asked but suddenly, they were listening to Jay speak with apprehension.

"Look, you piss fly, if you barely touch my breast, I will kill you when we get out of here! Do you hear me? Touch my breast and you are dead!" Jay threatened.

Without speaking, Lenny rolled closer to Jay. He opened his mouth and Jay looked away as she grabbed his false teeth, turned them over and removed the pin from what looked like a gaping hole which seemed predestined for concealment. Holding the false teeth and the pin precariously, since she could not bear to touch them, Jay looked at Lenny for her next instructions.

"Jay, don't you dare drop my teeth." Lenny first warned and carried on as he opened his mouth while speaking at the same time.

"Now kindly put my teeth back into my mouth and then I will tell you how to unpick your cage lock so that you can then do the same on all of ours." Lenny instructed.

"This is so gross. You need implants, man." Jay crossly moaned as she looked at Lenny's gums.

Turning her face away, Jay cautiously touched Lenny's lips and refitted his teeth. Kendal and Addison watched as if they were in the twilight zone.

Kendal felt sure that this was like falling into the lowermost level of the ocean to which light can't infiltrate!

He could not fathom these incredible occurrences. He just wanted it to be over. He was scared stiff of this frightening mess they were all in and had no idea what so ever as to what their next step would be.

Kendal and Addison watched as Lenny instructed Jay in the fine art of lock picking.

Lenny called the moves and Jay tried to perform the actions. This was exceedingly excruciating to watch and also painful to listen to the exchanges between these two sworn adversaries.

"I said firmly push and tilt to the left. What the hell is wrong with your hearing?" Lenny expressed his annoyance.

It was plainly over Jay's lack of skill in following his lock picking instructions. He continued directing and Jay fumbled along as best as she could to get the lock opened.

"You are a bloody dyslexic criminal! You don't know left from right." Jay argued as she frantically twisted and turned the pin. More agonizing pushing and pulling on the cage lock ensued. Then, suddenly the lock clicked and it opened.

Chapter Twenty-Two

Armed with the search warrant fifteen Special Operation Tactical Officers were about to descend on the Dragon Tooth Restaurant. It was closed because of the State of Emergency. The black tactical uniforms blended in well with the smoke laden atmosphere and the gradually blackening sky of London's city.

Riley led the charge as Landry reinforced the rear. The team was prepared with, firearms, tasers, batons, incapacity spray and most of all, courage to conduct this search. Riley and Landry had briefed the team about the use of the poison dart and the North Korean link. As such everyone had to be really careful.

Now arriving almost outside of the Dragon Tooth, they rapidly exited their vehicles and ran in tactical formation right up to the restaurant's entrance. Instantly, Riley banged on the door.

"Police! Police! Police! Open up!" Loud shouts bellowed from every team member. This was the way to disorient and divert the attention of those under suspicion.

More shouts continued but the door remained closed. Just as Riley was about to battery ram the door, it slowly opened. Riley was astonished to see Gang Fan standing with calm composure, his squinty eyes dimming.

"I am Detective Inspector Riley from the Metropolitan Police. Here's my identification." Riley stated and went on.

"I have a warrant to search these premises in regard to the murder of Kyong Rang who worked here." Riley informed.

"Are you Gang Fan, the owner of this establishment?" Riley inquired.

Gang Fan merely shook his head in what appeared to be an unconcerned acknowledgement and slowly stepped aside to allow them entry. Gang Fan watched them with a faceless expression.

Riley next gave Gang Fan a copy of the search warrant so that he would know what was going on. He took the paper and placed it on the bar. Riley further detailed what he wanted Gang Fan to do.

"Sir, I need you to verbally state your ownership of this establishment." Riley explained.

"Are you the owner of these premises?" Riley inquired.

"Ya, ya." Gang Fan confirmed.

"Is there anyone else present on these premises right now? If so, please let us know right now." Riley questioned.

Gang Fan looked at Riley once more and slowly shook his head from left to right. He did not answer as he looked around at each police officer.

"Please can you give a verbal confirmation that your answer is no." Riley asked.

"No, no." Gang Fan slowly replied.

"Please can you now step aside so that we may conduct the search?" Riley instructed.

The team swiftly moved about in the restaurant as Gang Fan sat on a bar stool being closely observed by two officers. The others went to work in conducting the in-depth search of the premises.

Landry and Riley delved into cupboards, boxes and stacks of items which were under counters but nothing was producing any kind of evidence which would suggest any illegal irregularities. Several plastic containers were filled with spices and herbs and on the face of things it was difficult to ascertain whether they were a threat. Landry had them marked to be taken away for further analysis.

"Now joining some other officers in the kitchen, Landry and Riley felt that they were becoming stumped; they looked around and then at each other.

"Landry, even this kitchen is cleaner than most, looks like he had a recent hygiene job carried out here." Riley observed.

"Possibly a fast clean up, to hide things?" Landry wondered as they walked to the back of the kitchen.

"Mighty big freezers for such a small restaurant." Riley observed as he opened the door to one of them and looked inside.

"I thought so too. These are usually found in large hotel kitchens." Landry noted as Riley walked and subsequently opened each freezer. He peered curiously inside and shifted the contents to the outside.

"Well, he has whole piglets in this one and the other two are stuffed with sides of beef and loads of chickens." Riley described.

"So, what the heck is going on with the Kyong Rang murder since this place is not revealing anything out of the ordinary." Landry pondered as he kept carefully looking around. Then a sergeant on the team approached them.

"Sir we have checked out back and in every section of the restaurant. All that is outback are six satellite dishes and nothing else." He informed them.

Riley thanked him and he walked back into the front of the restaurant. Riley then turned to Landry.

"Well, time to question father time." Riley unenthusiastically announced.

"That beard does look well lived in." Landry added. They walked disappointedly back out of the kitchen to interrogate Gang Fan but Landry stopped abruptly and turned back. Riley followed him out back once more and they went outside. Landry looked up and held a puzzled expression.

"Did you see any televisions inside, anywhere at all? Landry asked.

"Well no." Riley responded.

"So why in the hell does this place have all of these satellite dishes?" Landry wondered as he motioned to an officer who was standing out back.

"Bring Gang Fan out here, we will do the questioning right here." Landry requested.

The officer promptly went to fetch Gang Fan. Shortly, he had returned with the bearded old man. Gang Fan's beard was ahead of him and his eyes were dimmed. His presence seemed to hold extraordinary passive restraint. He looked as though he was experiencing a mind and body block.

"Do you have a television?" Landry began.

"No English. No speak English." Gang Fan replied.

Landry and Riley realized that they had overlooked requesting an interpreter but Landry laboured on since he was very much aware that the claim to not speaking English was a brilliant alibi in times such as these. Pointing to the satellite dishes Landry continued his probe.

"Up there, what are those used for? Why do you have them without any TV?" Landry loudly shouted as he stared down Gang Fan who also kept the cold stare.

Riley watched Landry and thought that when people claim not to be able to speak English, then it is possibly hoped that shouting will stand in as an interpreter. Landry was certainly fulfilling this view.

Gang Fan was unmoved as he continued to shake his head confirming that he could not understand what Landry was asking.

His darkened eyes were steely slits and they increased his unmoved demeanor. However, this was the only choice which Landry and Riley had, to believe his claim of his inability to communicate in English or to refute it.

His body language gave no clues whatsoever.

Turning away from Gang Fan to Riley, Landry consulted to make a decision concerning this impasse.

"Shall we call for an interpreter or shall we leave this alone and return if anything else crops up?" Landry asked.

Riley looked at Gang Fan and up at the satellite dishes. He breathed in and out as Landry waited for an answer.

Chapter Twenty-Three

For the moment, Kendal, Addison, Jay and Lenny had managed to gain limited freedom. They were out of their cages but remained imprisoned by the four cold walls. No windows. No doors. No way out. In these minutes, Kendal was firmly convinced that they were in a living hell. They huddled together to keep warm. Their eyes flitted about, and then Kendal spoke with deep desperation.

"We climbed up but my bet is that we are still under the Dragon Tooth" Kendal stated.

"This looks like there is nothing more to it but I get the feeling that this place has different levels, also them cages, bet that they keep dogs to go." Lenny angrily added.

Lenny then stood up and poked on the low and mucky ceiling. He was hitting it very hard and it was flaking off, bits were crumbling and falling.

"Shush! Shush." Kendal touched Lenny as he pointed to the other side of the ceiling that Lenny was about to touch.

"Do you hear that again?" Kendal asked. They all listened as an eerie tap was heard once more.

"This shit again!" Lenny snapped and went on.

"This ceiling feels soft; let's see if we can push it in." He suggested.

"You ain't got no idea what's up there! Don't!" Jay sharply objected.

"Well Miss Mona Lisa, why don't you try brainstorming and give us some really fast options!" Lenny fumed.

"If you push it, then it might cave in and kill us and besides they might be up there and catch us again." Jay sobbed.

Addison just held her close as if his arms could reassure her that all would be fine. He too had continuing doubts as to whether they would ever get out of this helix hellacious nightmare alive but he had to be strong for Jay.

"Jay just let's try it." Addison consoled as he hugged her tightly.

Lenny just watched with withheld annoyance and muttered under his breath to Kendal.

"It is a good thing that Jay wasn't alive and wasn't conscripted to the army back in 1939, otherwise Hitler would have fucking won!" Lenny whispered and then continued.

"Come on Kendal, let's push really hard. See it's giving in already." Lenny beamed.

And indeed, large flakes of the ceiling started to fall in their faces and onto their heads. Lenny and Kendal kept up the pressure.

"Push! Push harder!" Lenny cried.

As more and more flakes fell, Addison and Jay joined in, adding more power to bring down their roof of imprisonment. The falling pieces were a combination of sharp and damp boards which hit their half-naked torsos. Each push was increased, until dust and chips had covered their bodies. They wiped their eyes to gain sight from the blinding dust and continued the pushing.

"We are getting there; I can see some kind of light in this hole." Kendal reported as he stuck his face up closer.

"Push! Push!" Lenny urged as his hand went straight through a big chunk which subsequently fell right off and allowed them liberty from one section of their prison. They could hear the pronounced buzzing sound even more clearly now.

Lenny slowly pushed his dust covered face up through the opening and then instantly jumped back down and huddled on the ground. Sudden and uncontrollable fear seemed to be causing him to shake. Panic was now plastered right across his dusty face as he started to hyper ventilate.

"Lenny what did you see up there?" Kendal asked the trembling Lenny.

The others watched on in silent fear as they could well imagine that it had to be something awful to rack Lenny. His eyes blinked and then he spoke.

"That man, your boss, is up there, man." Lenny shakily replied.

Kendal looked up at the hole. No one moved.

"We were told that Jian was dead, burnt in the fire." Kendal whispered.

"Look for yourself." Lenny muttered as his body amplified its shaking.

Kendal was afraid if Jian was up there, then there were really in more than hell, he feared. He tried to move pass Lenny but Lenny suddenly grabbed his hand.

"Wait a minute, man don't go. Don't look." Lenny held Kendal's hand and continued to speak with real consternation on his face. Kendal could tell that whatever was up there was bad. Lenny was usually an unmovable rock but he was plainly scared right now.

"Your boss is dead, man! And hanging from the balls! A woman, a woman with her throat cut is also hanging." Lenny burst out and went on as they all listened in captive horrific quietness.

"The two bodies, all mutilated! All sliced up! A camera is rolling, some kinda ritualistic torture thing. What sick shit is this?" Lenny sputtered.

He retched as though he would be sick. They watched as the seconds passed and then Lenny spoke once more.

"You two stay here." Lenny ordered Jay and Addison and continued.

"Kendal, just let you and me go and see what else is up there." Lenny declared.

In a flash, Lenny didn't wait for an answer but got up and pulled Kendal behind him. Jay and Addison watched as the two disappeared up into the hole as the splinters of plaster fell from the ceiling covering their faces once more.

Addison looked at Jay as she cried and knew that the air had become even more strange and frightening but thinking of what was above was extremely spine-chilling and mind bending.

Chapter Twenty-Four

Up from hell but not out yet, Kendal and Lenny sneaked around taking care not to pass in front of the rolling camera. This was bizarre to say the least. Both Kendal and Lenny could not stomach to glance at the suspended bodies dangling in the air. Kendal felt that the woman looked like the one, who was taking the key from the plant pot, from the Google Street View of Jian's house.

These two young men maintained complete absence of sound. Like a SWAT team, face and hand gestures were all that they could use.

Pointing to the floor and to what looked like another trapped door they tiptoed and softly pulled on its recess. They quietly lifted the hatch and got on their bellies and peered down into this well lighted space. There was now a clear view of a stairway leading down to a lower room. This was incredible. As they bent over and gazed down, they could see stacks and stacks of equipment all neatly laid out.

On the side facing walls, screens that looked like computer monitors, were mounted on these walls; these monitors were all lit up. Kendal and Lenny stretched their bodies to the max but it was still very hard to tell what the displays were showing, without going down to them. There was also a constant loud buzz of noise which was being emitted.

Fighting back intense feelings of terror, Kendal and Lenny motioned to each other that they were going to go down. The two softly inched their way down the steps and looking up, suddenly Kendal saw what looked like another trapdoor, the one which he had, only had, a brief glimpse of when he had opened the freezer back in the Dragon Tooth restaurant's kitchen. His eyes widened and his heart fluttered wildly.

"Man, look at all this shit." Lenny whispered as their eyes had to absorb the massive amount of equipment.

"This looks like the Stock Exchange! Count these screens." Lenny softly called out.

"Lenny! Lenny, look closely at the screens." Kendal ordered.

"Fuck me! They are all showing London Streets and the underground. And what the hell is that loud buzzing?" Lenny whispered, as he looked around.

"Coming from that machine over there, look at all of those levers and dials, what is that very large machine controlling?" Kendal quizzed as they looked around more in search of any room cameras.

"Wow, man, this is something else." Lenny softly observed.

Not seeing any cameras, they walked over to take closer looks at what Kendal thought was extremely mysterious, unusual, surprising and difficult to understand or explain, technology, which filled the room. This room contained everything which constituted the unexplained.

"Look! Look. These screens show all military land and air defenses." Lenny pointed out as Kendal stared in amazement but then he managed to gather his words to form speech.

"That kitchen hand who was murdered, remember, he wrote the word 'steal' on that paper. He must have meant that this equipment was stolen." Kendal supposed.

"Man, those people English ain't good at all, so he possibly could not spell and wrote the wrong thing." Lenny replied as he kept looking at everything which the room contained in an effort to understand its purpose.

"Ohy! Ohy! Over here!" Lenny anxiously called out to Kendal.

"Look at this, a planning permission list of all buildings in London showing when they have been renovated or built." Lenny pointed out.

"What the fuck? What are they evaluating?" Lenny asked.

Kendal drew closer and looked at the documents. His brain was expanding at an alarming rate with information overload. He quickly scanned his eyes over the list.

"What does this all mean? It has to be connected to all the fires and attacks." Kendal supposed.

"Bet this would look really great on the International News, London taken out by a Chinese Take Away." Lenny commented.

"I can't really believe that, that bearded old man is behind all of this? What about Jian or whoever he was?" Kendal worriedly whispered.

Lenny kept on reading through papers and looking at screens. Kendal joined him in this reading race. He then stopped and looked at Lenny with great alarm scrawled on his face.

"What kinda shit are we in Lenny?" Kendal nervously asked as Lenny flipped paper after paper in a frantic dash to comprehend what was going on. Lenny then glanced at Kendal all the while still looking at the papers and then gave an answer.

"From the looks of all this, I would say, just like them bottom less drinks you get at Freddie's, then I would say, that we are in bottomless shit!" Lenny replied.

Following this exchange, the two pulled themselves away from the unexplained. Together they dashed about looking for some kind of clothes but could see none. Kendal knew that the second trap door which they could see, led directly into the Dragon Tooth but he had no idea how he would get it to open from this side. Nothing was visible. There was no handle to pull or slide.

The two stopped their search as the buzzing noise of the dials on the enormous machine turned and the buzzing got greater than before. They watched the rotation as it synchronized with the action on one of the large projected screens.

In total horror, right before their eyes Kendal and Lenny witnessed the complete destruction of Big Ben! It caught on fire and melted right before their eyes. The legs underneath them almost failed as this shocking event hit their system.

Gradually overcoming this, Lenny and Kendal knew that they had to do something but what? The two slowly looked at each other and then at the death machine. Moving slowly towards it, their eyes dilated with misgivings about how to disable it.

"Kendal, did you just see Big Ben destroyed? Or did I dream all of this?" Lenny questioned.

"Lenny it is this machine, I am sure that is responsible for these explosions." Kendal said and continued.

"Let's get Addison and Jay up here so that they can help us work this out." Kendal reasoned.

"What? Mona Lisa will get in the way with doomsday predictions!" Lenny resisted.

He looked at Kendal as though he had sentenced him to death.

"No, we need help and they will be worried as to what has happened to us." Kendal countered.

"Well captain, you go get them and hope that that bearded old man don't come and gut us like fish." Lenny warned as he resumed sifting through all that was on the counters and tables in the room.

"I will be right back; just don't touch any of those computers or machines!" Kendal cautioned.

As he swiftly and noiselessly passed, what remained of his former boss, gigantic swells of adrenaline rushed through every organ in his body. He now rapidly slid back down through the hole and landed on the cold ground.

Jay and Addison were huddled in a corner and held a cage as a weapon in case they were confronted by their enemies.

"No time to explain but we all have to go through that hole. An awful sight of Jian and a woman is up there so don't look." Kendal warned and continued.

"Don't make a sound either a camera is rolling. Come on." Kendal ordered.

"Is there a way out up there?" Jay asked as her wobbly legs struggled to stand. Kendal just paused and looked at her. Maybe Lenny was right but he shrugged this thought off.

"Jay it will be fine. Come on." Addison reassured.

Kendal's mind was working overtime trying to comprehend everything which it was now about to suffer a break down from if they did not get out of this place soon.

Kendal climbed through the hole first, followed by Addison and then they pulled Jay up. Kendal put his hand to his lips indicating silence. As they slowly moved, Jay caught sight of Jian's body and started to retch violently. Addison put his hand over her mouth to suppress the urging noises as the last remaining contents of her stomach were pouring out.

Very soon they reached the other side and quickly got down the steps to join Lenny. There was a lone chair with a cotton cloth covered seat. They all watched as Lenny took the chair up, bit into the material and then started to strip the cloth covering. He then offered the ripped cloth covering to Jay to wrap around her chest to return some semblance of dignity to her.

"Thanks Lenny, thanks." Jay softly said and straight away started to wrap herself.

"Now, don't let me have to take back that cloth and use it as a gag on you." Lenny cautioned.

"We have to keep our guard up looking out for that chef and the bearded old man." Kendal told them and went on to explain what they had to do.

"Addison, if you and Jay would keep your eyes on that trapdoor over there. I think that is the one which goes up through the freezer into the Dragon Tooth's kitchen." He outlined.

"Just hold that old chair over it so that it will give me and Lenny some time to run over and help. They won't be expecting that we have got out of the cages." Kendal detailed as Lenny took the chair and held it in the direction of Addison and Jay.

"I would really like to do the same to them two! Cage their asses!" Lenny whispered.

Addison then moved to take the chair while Jay just stared at Kendal and Lenny, only slowly moving over to help Addison. Lenny then swiftly ran over to the massive machine.

"Over here Kendal. This monster machine is controlled by some kind of computer programme." Lenny informed and continued.

"From looking at those screens I think that they are showing the London land marks that are to be hit and the machine is responding by activating the destruction sequence." Lenny supposed.

"Lenny, I think that is correct but we still do not know exactly how it is all executed. How the detonation is actually carried out." Kendal added and like lightning he went and grabbed the planning list which they had looked at earlier.

"This list I feel has something extra special in significance. Why not just blow up any old city buildings that have been there for centuries?" Kendal asked.

"Well, they just did, Big Ben." Lenny said. "Yeah, but there are bigger fish in this city pond, like

Buckingham Palace." Kendal argued as he continued to look at the list.

"Every one of these buildings has been refurbished. Big Ben was repaired just a few years ago, Tower Bridge and Admiralty Arch, also." Kendal specified as Lenny listened.

"All of them had work done on them so how does that connect them for being blown to pieces?" Kendal wondered.

"A construction worker with a big grudge? One who didn't get paid?" Lenny quipped.

"What's bothering me is all of this technology in this room and the fact that the buildings all melted." Kendal deliberated.

"That melting is some weird shit but look out in that other space out there, your boss hanging by the balls; that woman cut to shreds; man, that is all weird shit too!" Lenny asserted and continued.

"Then blowing that poison dart into-"Lenny was abruptly stopped by Kendal.

"Yeah, you hit the nail on the head, supposed these Dragon Tooth people had somehow placed something into, inside, the building materials which were used to repair, renovate and build all of these structures?" Kendal supposed.

"Man, that is some real deep shit Kendal, but how would it not be spotted? There is an inspection of everything in this country, even for loo roll! Man, if the British had landed on the moon first, instead of planting the flag, they would've looked at the ground and shouted, stop! Jagged surface, danger! So how would anything get pass the health and safety police here?" Lenny queried.

"I don't know but when we were in that police van that sergeant said that no one knew how the explosions started and were baffled by the melting so my view could be correct." Kendal reiterated and pushed on.

"Now what's in all of these buildings?" Kendal asked.

"Well bricks, water. I ain't ever worked in construction. Too much energy, too little money! Man, I ain't that strong." Lenny replied.

"Lenny, steel, steel, is in all of those buildings to make them strong." Kendal asserted as if a light bulb had been switched on in his head. He looked at

Lenny for encouragement but Lenny was unconvinced that this was the golden key.

"That kitchen hand's note said steal. Don't you remember?" Kendal expectantly waited but Lenny brushed it off.

"Man, I tell you that that kitchen hand could not write good English and he was all mixed up, not to mention, on his last breath." Lenny reasoned and went on.

"Look, at these." Lenny pointed to two screens with aerial views and Kendal picked up on these.

"Lenny, I feel that all this surveillance feeds back to that machine over there." Kendal pointed out and rushed over to the machine once more. Jay then turned, walked quickly and looked anxiously at the machine. She next spoke.

"Is there a phone in here?" She nervously queried.

"If there was, we would have used it already." Lenny fumed and went on.

"Yeah, Jay, we are all just here on a short city break, taking it easy, just chilling out, almost naked as we were born! Pretending we are at the beach." Lenny sarcastically remarked and carried on.

"Ain't, you supposed to be helping Addison hold that trapdoor? So why the hell you over here?" Lenny seethed.

There and then, Kendal knew that he had to intervene and so he quickly spoke to everyone.

"OK, let's all calm down. We are all in this together so let's try to get out of it together and in one piece." Kendal sighed and turned to Lenny yet again.

"I am damn sure that that kitchen hand meant to tell me something about steel and because his English wasn't good, he wrote steal. It has to be that there is something in the steel which is in all of those buildings." Kendal reckoned.

He now watched as Jay began pacing back and forth and they all could tell that one of her panic attacks was coming. Addison tried to hug and walk with her but tripped and knocked over the chair. It made the most horrendous noise. They all did fast freeze and even their eyes were stone.

At once the mysterious room revealed yet another part of its secret character. They watched in liquefied fright, which dripped from their bodies in the form of intense perspiration, as another concealed trapdoor flew open and in rushed the chef!

This time he had someone gripped by the hair and dragging behind him. Their chilled blood gurgled so loudly, that it drowned out thoughts and action. Kendal was certain that his blood had been completely drained from his body.

Chapter Twenty-Five

Several hours had passed and after waiting for an interpreter to attend at the Dragon Tooth. Landry and Riley had now left the Dragon Tooth with hands filled with emptiness. Gang Fan had insisted through the interpreter, that he had found the satellite dishes there when he took ownership of the property.

They were driving with speed when they were radioed and informed that they had to return to Scotland Yard pronto since the Prime Minister had received a demand from the attacker after the fall of Big Ben.

There was an un-surrendered quiet in the car even though they had not made any progress on this lead. Landry and Riley would not stop resisting this unknown enemy; this faceless and shadowless opponent had to be stopped but how?

"What do you suppose the demand is and who is it coming from?" Landry queried.

"Don't let's speculate we are almost at headquarters." Riley answered.

They drove the remaining short distance being held in subdued space. Soon the vehicle was parked and they rushed to the Cobra Defense Committee meeting, to hear about the demand. Entering the Commissioner's office, they sat once more with the chiefs and heads of all national services. The Commissioner stood with a remote control in his hand and addressed everyone.

"This is a very sad hour. The Prime Minister has received via a video broadcast an ultimatum." The Commissioner coughed and looked around the room.

"Our Prime Minister has been given until 1800 hours, three hours from now, to relinquish British Sovereignty." The Commissioner paused as if a weight had been thrown on his head and then went on.

"The right and power of our country to govern ourselves has been demanded to be handed over at 1800 hours. The Prime Minister has yet to be informed as to the identity of the person making the demands." The Commissioner could hear the screaming silence of those in the room. He waited for questions.

"We do not know who is making the demand?" Landry asked.

"No. The voice was disguised and only a black facial outline was shown." The Commissioner replied and went on.

"We are working feverishly to locate the place of origin where the video broadcast streamed from." He added.

"What will result if this demand is not met?" Riley asked.

Everyone stared at the Commissioner with undecided emotions.

"The answer to that question and others can be found in this video." He stated as his eyes flit about.

The Commissioner subsequently turned to the large projected screen and switched it on. They all silently watched. The video commenced its play.

"Good day Prime Minister. I am sure that my little displays across your city and within your strategic defenses, have been impressive but not as impressive as this." The voice gloated.

Then the video switched to a scene of epic destruction. It was a simulation of the explosion of the Sizewell Nuclear Power Station in the East of England. The distorted voice then continued.

"That little show of Sizewell will help you to make a speedy decision. Also at random times, leading up 1800 hours, one of your city buildings across the entire country, will be destroyed. Hope you liked how Big Ben went at 1400 hours." The distorted voice stated and carried on.

"I will be waiting to hear from you, just press the play button on this video at 1800 hours as the confirmation of your surrender or Sizewell will be your ultimate undoing." The voice abruptly stopped and the screen then went blank.

There was a tremendous buzz in the room, exacerbated by the knowledge that they had not been able to identify their unknown foe; suddenly the room fell into dark quietness. The Commissioner next separated the stillness.

"We have to do something to prevent this from getting to the media and panicking the population." The Commissioner stated.

"The Prime Minister will address the nation in one hour but we have absolutely nothing to fight this with." The Military General added.

"Where is this might and strength being operated from?" The Commissioner demanded. All eyes around the room circled. They were lots of questions but very few answers.

"We are dealing with a ruthless person who seems to be in a powerful position, with Britain in their hands. We would never submit to this authority, what or whoever this person is." The Commissioner affirmed.

"That North Korean man that was murdered, Kyong Rang? What is happening with that line of investigation?" The Commissioner demanded.

"We attended the premises where he worked and have only just returned but we have not gathered anything of significance." Riley informed.

All eyes watched Landry and Riley as if stripping them of any useable information.

"How did we get to this? How?" The Commissioner questioned. Just then, there was a knock at the door.

"Yes? Come." The Commissioner called out and an Inspector entered.

"Sir, I must ask you to switch on the television. We just had reports from the BBC that their channels have been taken over and a broadcast is about to start." The Inspector reported.

He then, rapidly walked and turned the television on. He stepped back, as everyone looked on at BBC channel 101.They now heard the identical distorted voice from the video to the Prime Minister.

"We interrupt your viewing to give you an important message. People of Britain, I will soon be your new leader, this is an advanced broadcast to you." The warped voice proclaimed and continued.

"At 1800 hours today, your country will surrender willingly and peacefully or unwillingly and deadly! We will then identify who we are." The voice firmly stated.

"Your Prime Minister has just two hours and thirty minutes to make that decision." The screen next went black.

"Whoever he is, he beat us to it. The Prime Minister has to get on the air pronto. There will be gross panic in the country." The Commissioner raged.

Just then another report came in that the London Gherkin was gone, completely melted!

"Landry, Riley, you and your team, you have to find out where this all is being supported and shut it down! Now!" The Commissioner thundered.

Chapter Twenty-Six

Choosing to live or die could never be an easy decision, even if a suicide act was contemplated so as to save other lives. Therefore, Kendal knew that he was faced with this short straw task, if any of them were going to leave the Dragon Tooth's dungeon alive. Only one thing was good about this harrowing situation, Sage was alive. She was quite drugged and dazed but alive. Jay was comforting her and they all huddled together to keep warm.

The chef had dragged her from her make-shift prison after he had heard the noisy commotion, believing that the police had discovered their high-tech room. She was going to be used as a bargaining chip for freedom. Initially she was held by the man they knew as Jian, in that hammock under his Duck Lane place. This explained the tapping which they had heard. Kendal still had to understand how she got there in the first instance. Hopefully he would live to find out.

"I don't like problems. You all have caused us great problems." The chef angrily looked at them and loudly complained.

Kendal could see that the chef had a transparent sling bag around his neck. From the looks of it, it contained what looked like darts. Apart from these, he was not carrying any other overt weapon, only his size and weight. As he walked around the room in an intimidating fashion, Kendal fixed his eyes on Lenny. A diversion was needed to bring this beast down.

"Oh my God! Oh my God!" Lenny cried out and fell to the ground rolling over in pain. He clutched his stomach and raved on. The chef quickly turned to see what was happening with Lenny. Kendal and Addison took the chance to grab him. They jumped on his back and pushed him to the floor as they banged his head several times onto the hard surface.

Lenny sprinted up from his artificial agony and joined this strategic attack. The chef was strong and resisted this battery of blows and was able to turn his body facing upwards.

Pulling on the now visible sling bag, Lenny fought directly with the chef. As Kendal and Addison hit him, he concentrated on pounding Lenny with blows to stop him getting the poison bag. Lenny bit the strap to set the bag free but it was trapped under the weight of the chef's head.

Addison and Kendal tried to raise the chef's head so that Lenny could get the bag but he headbutted Kendal and bit Addison, but Lenny held on to the sling part of the bag. The chef then rolled over, his face bloodied and then managed to stumble and stand.

He suddenly grabbed Addison by the neck. Kendal punched his side but he held on to Addison as though in a vice grip. He swung Addison around like a rag doll in an effort to break his neck. Lenny grabbed the sling bag as he and Kendal hit him repeatedly in the head but his grip was a strong and evil hold. Suddenly Jay entered this death fight.

"Let him go you stinking animal!" Jay flew up and scratched the chef in his face. She dug her finger nails deep into his eyes, while Lenny kicked him in the testicles, until he released Addison. Jay quickly pulled Addison away and dragged him to the side of this fray.

While briefly recovering from this onslaught, the chef staggered, raised his legs and charged at Lenny and Kendal in a wild attempt to knock them to the floor.

In what appeared to be frame by frame motion, Kendal could see Lenny fumbling with the sling bag as this last dash would have meant touch down for the chef.

Lenny's hands and lips met as he blew one of the darts straight at the Chef, bull's eye! The dart hit him between the eyes. Kendal rejoiced, as the evil chef curled like a beached whale and slumped to the floor.

"Addison! Addison! Man, are you alright?" Kendal rushed to him and quickly asked.

"Yeah man, no worries." He painfully tried to groan away the fear. Jay sat and hugged him as tears fell out of her eyes.

With no time for recovery from this deadly skirmish, they all prepared for their next enemy but first they really needed to be warm.

"Quick, let's strip him. His clothes are huge; they can be torn and we each can have a piece to wrap ourselves in." Kendal reasoned as Lenny commenced the undressing.

"Man, this guy ate more than he served. Look at this blubber." Lenny observed as he, Kendal and

Addison pulled off the chef's clothes. His weight was phenomenal and they struggled to shift him around.

"Hum, hum, doesn't he look like he needs ironing? That is some massive cellulite man! May I never eat so many chocolates ever again!" Lenny exclaimed.

Minutes passed and they each had a piece of clothing wrapped around them to give at least a little relief from the cold. Their bodies now partially covered were still shaking from shock and fright but Kendal took charge once more.

"We need you and Jay to really keep guard at that door. The bearded old man will surely come back here." Kendal implored Addison and Jay.

"Why can't we just try to get away right now?" Jay pleaded.

"We can't just walk through that trapdoor because Sage cannot walk. One of us will have to lift her." Kendal paused. By this time Addison was holding Jay close and she was crying. Sage had lapsed into unconsciousness once more as Kendal hugged her and propped her head up as best as he could. Jay then released Addison and went over to Sage.

"The bearded old man is probably keeping guard and most of all, we have to find out how to stop that deadly machine." Kendal concluded.

By this time Lenny had already gone back to the large machine and was overlooking everything.

"If we pull all of these plugs what might happen?" Lenny asked.

"Don't!" Kendal almost screamed.

"Most of these things have booby traps, a device or setup that is planned to kill, if unknowingly activated by the actions of the victim." Kendal worriedly outlined.

Then he fell into profound thought which carried him back to his school days of science classes. He felt that the murdered kitchen hand really meant steel rather than steal but how could the steel in the buildings be affected? How? Kendal kept interrogating himself.

After a brief few minutes Lenny's voice shook Kendal from his extensive pit of thoughts. Kendal was startled by Lenny's excited but yet extremely nervous tone and he quickly rushed to get closer to what Lenny was looking at and describing.

"These levers on this machine are probably some band widths of some type of signal that is being sent out." Lenny proposed.

"Kendal, don't you remember seeing all those satellite dishes at the back of this place when we left the kitchen yesterday?" Addison queried and carried on.

"So, the signal maybe going out through those." Addison suggested.

"But what is the signal connected to and what is it doing to destroy big strong buildings?" Kendal questioned and continued.

"I am still on that s-t-e-a-l trail and I do feel that it's s-t-e-e-l." Kendal reiterated and spelt out the two words. He looked at his friends and now listened to Addison.

"Remember when we were in the store on Saturday, that some people were arguing that their pots and pans had melted. I would assume that these were stainless steel." Addison backed up Kendal.

"That signal machine thing, is my baby. I am following that." Lenny affirmed and carried on inspecting the machine.

"How about if this killer machine was linked to a satellite?" Lenny queried.

"You maybe on to something Lenny, satellites are usually free from outside control and are computer-controlled systems. Look around in here." Kendal added and went on.

"Satellites control things like, power generation, telemetry, thermal control, attitude control and orbit control." Kendal described.

"Some of them things you just called out, way too high above my hair but what if the satellite was being instructed to blow up and melt these buildings?" Lenny queried.

"Back to my steel theory, then there would have to be something already planted in the steel for the beam to the satellite, to activate in the steel, which would ultimately cause explosive action." Kendal reasoned.

"Shush, Shush!" Addison whispered. They all stopped and listened in poised readiness for another attack. Seconds passed but no one appeared. Breathing out they continued searching the room for answers as to how to stop this, when another explosive blast was screened, it was Westminster Abbey.

"Why would that man write a clue which spelt steal? It has to be the steel in these buildings." Kendal was at it again he just won't let his theory go.

"OK, Kendal let's examine this steel business." Lenny said.

They drew closer to the colossal contraption.

"First almost all steel for building anything is imported so even though it meets all the standards, suppose a component is added that goes undetected." Kendal assumed and carried on.

"So, let's suppose that this machine here sends up a signal to the satellite. The satellite relays it to the steel in the building and somehow breaks up the steel but how does the holy melt down occur?" Kendal wondered as he swiftly poured over information on the computers.

"Don't forget, most likely, that them melted pots and pans that Addison talked about were imported stainless steel too." Lenny added.

"So, who would stand to gain from all of this shit?" Lenny asked as he too kept on looking over information on the computers.

"I can't speak Chinese, well Mandarin or whatever language this is written in, but look at this picture on this laptop." Kendal told Lenny.

"You expect that I can read Chinese?" Lenny responded. He then left what he was looking through and dashed over to Kendal.

Kendal moved slightly so that Lenny could see the picture on the screen. Lenny's eyes widened and his jaw dropped almost to his chin. He looked at Kendal and then again at the screen. They both looked at each other with eyes staring.

"Fuck me! Ain't that, that, North Korean leader hugging fat cheeks, now dead over there? Mr. Chef? Man, the two look like relatives." Lenny reckoned and carried on.

"Fuck me! We in more bottomless shit than ever now!" Lenny declared.

"Now do you understand my speculations about that steel thing?" Kendal presumed as he had Lenny and Addison's undivided attention. Their looks seemed to be rapidly turning from anger to horrified shock.

"Now if we put that bearded old man with the two of these, we just saw in that picture, it would make a bad ass oil painting all made in China!" Lenny stated and carried on wildly.

"The Chinese are great pals with North Korea. They're in each other's underpants and put the two together, what a fucking big ass friendship!" Lenny stated.

"Fast! We have to figure out how to stop this machine." Kendal declared, as he and Lenny set to work to stop the devil's monstrous minions.

Chapter Twenty-Seven

Landry and Riley walked from the Cobra Defense Committee meeting and their heads were reeling. The division was alight with heated emotions seeping through uniforms. All these Cobra team officers had set lines of investigation to follow; therefore, conversation was absent. Everyone was busy grabbing at shreds of air, not even straw, was available in this evidence void investigation only their hair that was growing very thin!

"Landry, Riley!" Grimes urgently called out preventing them from walking to their office.

"Yes Grimes." Riley answered.

"We've got a fix on the location of that police radio." He informed.

"Where?" Landry asked.

"Dean Street, the Dragon Tooth Restaurant." Grimes anxiously stated.

"Are you sure?" Riley asked and went on.

"We were there already today and our search turned up nothing." Riley replied.

"Send one of the officers who are in the area. Let them take a look." Landry instructed.

"Right, Inspector Landry." Grimes replied.

"Wait what's the matter with you, Grimes?" Landry inquired.

"Nothing, Inspector Landry." Grimes answered once more.

"Oh, come on, you feel that we should go back there. That's what it is, isn't it?" Landry questioned as Riley watched.

"Well, yes, I do think that you should go back but you are the Inspector." Grimes pointed out and held down his head. Both Landry and Riley looked at Grimes' face.

"OK. Let's go Riley, chasing off after bloody straws while losing our hair." Landry specified.

"Well, this maybe the last freedom which we have chasing straws but may loss all of our hair. Don't you get severe punishment for failure over in North Korea, like death?" Riley grunted and went on.

"We are failing, you know. That faceless person may very well be whom we have to work for soon." Riley supposed as the two men got into their vehicle and left the station.

The drive was somber; the streets were bare except for armed officers. Dust clouds filled the atmosphere as the evening was closing in and the deadline was drawing near.

Riley looked around inside the vehicle, like the way things were right now, everything looked black inside. Black dash, black floor, black carpet, black radio, black broadcasts!

This ride was not a high-speed chase with flashing lights, just a deliberate drive to search and question. Riley and Landry listened as over their black radio; they received a status report. It was another black update that two tube stations had been destroyed and St Paul's Cathedral now also joined the destruction queue.

Deliberate ruin was placing its signature everywhere in the city and leaving an inheritance of sorrow on the hearts and minds of many. These two officers were beginning to feel powerless.

In a short while they had reached the Dragon Tooth. The entire place now looked even more deserted as they walked just in ordinary uniform, no special gear; the two Inspectors soon reached the door. They knocked but there was no answer. They knocked again but the same prevailed.

"Shall we check the back?" Riley asked.

"We might as well." Landry replied.

The two officers walked around to the adjacent street in order to access the back of the Dragon Tooth. They reached the rear entrance and could see a glimmer of light just peeping under the back door.

"I thought that Gang Fan lived here. There is no other address listed for him." Landry stated.

"Seems very deserted; maybe he is meditating." Riley speculated and went on.

"Strangely enough, we never saw any sleeping quarters in there when we searched." Riley pointed out.

"Possibly he has a fold away bed or sleeps on the floor." Landry reckoned.

"Then we should have seen the bed." Riley reflected as his senses were aroused.

"Tiredness can compromise thinking." Landry said and went on.

"There was nothing that we saw but then again the obvious sometimes stares us in the face." Landry lamented.

"We both are still tired so these things happen." Riley apologized as they knocked at the back door.

"So, no answer at the front and now no answer at the back. Where could he have gone, given that there is a state of emergency?" Riley wondered.

"The search warrant is still valid so we can enter if we feel that he poses a threat and may have an officer abducted." Landry detailed.

They then started to look around the rubbish bins to see if by chance the police radio was thrown into one. Nothing was in the bins. As they both looked around more, suddenly they heard the faint sound of a gunshot. The two stopped in their tracks and held their weapons.

"Did you hear that?" Riley whispered.

"Sounded as though it came from somewhere below but when we searched, there was no basement." Landry responded and activated his radio.

"Back up needed at 44 Dean Street, Dragon Tooth Restaurant, China Town. Shots heard at rear of building!" Riley boomed into the speaker.

With weapons drawn, Riley and Landry crouched, eyes alerted and waited for their tactical backup to arrive. In what seemed like an eternity, but was only minutes, the police sirens could be heard in the distance. Soon as they got nearer the sounds died but were rapidly replaced by the loud slamming of vehicle doors.

Feet thumping, boots hitting the ground hard, officers spread like a swarm. Black tactical gear was filled with countless combatants who had now converged on the Dragon Tooth restaurant!

The entire building was completely surrounded. With backup in place, Riley banged on the door and announced their presence once more.

"Police! Police! Police!" They barked.

Once again there was no response. Landry broke the door's lock and Riley backed up Landry as Landry cautiously eased in.

"Police! Gang Fan. Police!" Landry bellowed.

Then Riley stealthy entered followed by other team officers. With weapons drawn, they spread out to look all around, pulling furniture and overturning boxes. Drawing closer to Landry Riley questioned.

"Have you seen a bed or any sleeping space?" Riley probed.

"No just as before, nothing has been revealed but where did the shot come from?" Landry queried and turned to the tactical team.

"Team, turn this place upside down. Look for hidden walls or trap doors, anything which might show concealment to another space." Riley thundered.

The team promptly and zealously set about searching, knocking walls, tapping floors and hitting the ceiling; eyes were in x-ray mode. Every section of the restaurant was saturated with delving hands. They looked all around but could not find any presence of anything or anyone.

Chapter Twenty-Eight

Kendal, Addison, Lenny, Jay and Sage had not been able to keep Gang Fan out of the room. He had discharged a shot down through the trap door grazing Addison in the process. Gang Fan, the one known to them as the bearded old man, now stood facing them with the gun fastened to Sage's head. Sage was so out of it from being drugged, that she could barely open her eyes.

"You meddling prats! You think you can stop this." The bearded old man declared as he threw Sage back to the ground.

Kendal was shocked at how good his English had suddenly become but even more surprised when he threw off the long beard and his face was identical to the Jian Ling's photo, that the police had shown them Friday night in the mobile unit!

What Kendal also could not know was, that this face that was now revealed, was also the face of the supposed rice farmer in Shanghai. He certainly was not in a paddy field. He now walked around encircling them and waving the gun as he dragged Sage.

"I am your nastiest nightmare! You want to play brave but you will fear the pain of those you love." Gang Fan menacingly threatened as he looked at Sage and then at Jay. Kendal and all the others watched as Gang Fan stopped, pushed Sage down and grabbed Jay by the neck.

"Leave her alone you filthy animal!" Addison shouted as the three young men lurched forward.

"Stop or she dies now!" He threatened as he held Jay tightly with the gun to her head.

"You have pissed me off and I never take out a worthy opponent until they cease to try, so move again!" He threateningly warned and went on as he evilly looked at the young men and then at Sage who was passed out. Jay started to wail loudly as her panic was seeping out of her frightened body.

"Whose loved one, is she? Ah but you're not going to speak." He laughed and shook his head.

"You see, loved ones are fair game. I get great pleasure in taking one of your pawns off this board game; it's the game called life!" He loudly laughed again.

"You're insane." Kendal said as his fear now turned to heated anger.

This madman quickly swung Jay around as she sobbed and clutched her chest to keep it covered. He glared and shouted out.

"Economics and strategy games are the games I like best. The ones involving scarce resources and strategy! Yes, I love games. Don't you all?" His menacing laugh bounced out again as he carried on.

"You all like Monopoly?" He taunted and menacingly glared at them.

"You should know that the purpose of Monopoly is to bankrupt your opponents and get the maximum money at the end of the game." He sneered. As he dragged Jay around, he stared them in the eye. He then dimmed his eyes, kicked a box and carried on.

"Don't let yourself get bankrupt, use strategy." He scoffed and laughed once more.

"Implement a high-level scheme to accomplish one or more of your goals, under conditions of great uncertainty. That's strategy! Your country loves strategic games! Mine, loves schemes!" He mocked.

"Well, I guess, that our numbers are up so since you are going to kill us, just tell us some more about your plot." Kendal snapped.

"I would be disappointed if you weren't convinced that you all are going to die. So, I guess, a last wish can be granted." He laughed and dragged Jay to the huge machine.

"Let me tell you this story. In my country we tell our children long stories, the ones which they keep in their minds to develop strategy over opponents or let's say, allies." He outlined and laughed again.

"To our advantage in time there have been many changes to the way steel is made. Cheap steel helped start the Industrial Revolution right here in your country." He snickered and carried on.

"Don't go to sleep now, stories make you young people sleepy, bored. That is why you don't' get so many stories being told in your country but they are told in mine. No handing down of important information, here. You, young people get too much choice. Stand upright! No slouching!" He ordered them, and continued.

"Steel is used in making almost everything, very versatile, isn't it?" He remarked.

"Now the great part; steel is a metal alloy, with iron, carbon and atoms. Some atoms hold together quite well, which is what makes some solid materials really hard." He coughed, shook Jay to an upright position once more.

Her eyes were spent from the tears shed. She just closed her puffy red eye balls and held her head down. He shook her and shook her, as though she was a stuffed doll.

"Up! Head up! You must listen!" He shouted at Jay and pulled her neck up into a straight position and carried on.

"Now my partners on the export side, know that altering the amount of carbon and other atoms added to steel, will change those things that are valuable and really needed in the steel." He grinned.

Kendal could see that delight radiated in his face. Then while pointing the gun at Jay's head, he swiftly looked at Lenny and caught him glaring in anger.

"Don't you dare frown at me or you will get the pleasure of forced Hari- Kari!" He loudly shouted and carried on.

"Just like those two hanging out there, with the camera rolling for all to see, is exactly what happens, when you try to cross me!" He shouted.

"Go fuck yourself!" Lenny angrily exploded and lunged at him. He stepped back and furiously spoke again.

"Don't you worry; I might just do it to you before I cut your head off and shit down your throat!" He retorted.

"Go on tell us what you did to the steel." Kendal butt-in, in an effort to diffuse the scorching exchanges between this madman and Lenny.

"Smart man, you are trying to save your friend, clever move." He remarked and carried on.

"Now your steel comes to you in high grade very nice. Passes all standards, that's really how good we are." The young men eyed him but he shook Jay more and pressed the gun to her temple. He boasted on as he turned his eyes towards the monstrous machine.

"But my Su Ling here, what a big-time boss!" He bragged, laughed and carried on as he used the gun to tap on the dials of the awful monster machine.

"Just the turn of these dials, all computer controlled, will send a sonic beam through those satellites dishes up to one of our 80 orbiting satellites in the sky." He declared.

"Starry night, beautiful sky, you look up and think. Our satellite will then relay that sonic beam to anyone of your prized buildings which have our steel in it and zap!" He pointed out as he stood and looked from one to the other, with pleasurable destruction, incased in his face.

"See the star, that really bright satellite in the sky? Our sonic beam ruptures the crystalline structure in the already compromised steel which your buildings are made structurally sound with. And what a bang! What trust! What a mighty melt down!" He loudly cheered.

"But what about the melted stainless-steel pots and pans? Why hit those?" Kendal queried.

"That is to show that we can destroy anything, anywhere, any of our exports." He beamed.

"What do you get from hurting innocent people?" Kendal harshly queried.

"The pleasure of being a leader within a great and new empire, the takeover of Britain by North Korea!" He roared and carried on.

"Today at 1800 hours, there will be a new player on the world stage." He beamed.

"Now you get the chance to pick the next melting spot. Come here." He directed this command to Kendal, who had no choice but to obey. He subsequently then instructed. He pointed to a city map displayed on a screen on the wall.

"Choose between Scotland Yard and The Royal Courts of Justice. Your lucky pick today!" He laughingly thundered.

"Go on. Go on. It's your city so you get to call this score; we can add to the sequence of hits." He barked in a coarse tone as he shoved Kendal with his foot.

Incensed by this horror, Kendal looked at Lenny and facial gestures said it all. It was now or never to get out of this dead pool. As the man's out stretched foot kicked Kendal once more, like a footballer, Kendal tackled him.

He lost his footing and Lenny rushed in, like a defending goal keeper and kicked his other leg which sent him reeling to the ground.

Jay fell on the side of him, and he scrambled to keep hold of her. Addison pulled her free and Lenny rushed in again with kicks to the head and face. In this heated melee, Kendal searched for the gun but the man still had it, it was lodged under his leg.

Lenny spotted the gun and he and Kendal quickly jumped to roll the man over to force out the gun. The man rolled and slipped from their grasp. He scrambled to his feet and threw a punch; it hit Kendal right in the face. He staggered back away from the man, but he levelled a kick and knocked Kendal to the ground. Lenny could see what was happening but he was still fumbling to get the gun which had by now rolled under the big machine.

Kendal raised himself up but the man quickly moved in and grabbed him but Kendal's bare back slipped from his grasp. Addison joined the fight and jumped on the man's back but was flung like a feather through the air and laid unconscious on the ground. Jay ran and was sobbing over him.

Kendal threw punches but missed the man's face; he ducked and advanced with punches to Kendal's waist. As he pulled Kendal to him and gripped his waist, he was contorting and twisting Kendal's body in every direction possibly to place it in a bear hug. Kendal turned and punched but to no avail, the man's strength was remarkable.

"Let me go! You bloody pig!" Kendal shouted as he struggled and struggled while the man squeezed and crushed. He felt his ribs separating within his chest. At any moment air would be forced from his lungs and his ribs would be expelled. Kendal glanced around seeking help and at last he noticed that Lenny had reached the gun. Lenny held it in his shaking hands. Then he pointed and aimed but it wobbled about.

Lenny knew that he had to take the chance and fire; he prayed that his aim would not fail. He closed one eye and then he fired a shot. The recoil unbalanced him but both the struggling and squeezing, had now stopped, as Kendal and the once bearded old man tumbled lifeless to the ground.

Chapter Twenty-Nine

In the meanwhile, floor boards of the Dragon Tooth restaurant, were being ripped up, walls were being smashed in as Laundry and Riley's frantic eyes searched all around. Then, Laundry's phone rang, interrupting this probe and he could see that it was a video call. He stared at the screen as Riley joined him; their eyes were now fixed on the live stream. To their horror, it was a broadcast which was showing what could only be a macro hell.

Fierce floods of flames were completely swamping Westminster Abbey! Numerous people were gathered there, in pray for the city. The detectives stared at the violent explosions that rent the air, as if they were bent on crushing life, by ripping apart every atom in the atmosphere! Throngs of people were fleeing with bright hot flames glowing from their bodies, which seemed to be ignited by gas, that was generated by a hellacious combustible source, as never seen before!

The detectives' eyes were attached to a scene too incredible to be believed. The flames were consuming the whole building and everyone with intent on reducing everything to ashes. Riley held his head as he sadly thought, that the deathly screams expressed, the intent, that the heat radiating all around, was an anger, and thirst for destruction, that appeared to be a terrible joy of some sick and twisted soulless individual. His sadness switched to anger, as he felt that it was, as if the fire, was the reflection of the arsonist, some kind of broken individual, who wanted no more than to destroy for pleasure and joy.

They watched on in revulsion and holy terror, as the Abbey that stood for over seven hundred years, held the buried souls of thousands, including Elizabeth I and the artist and dramatist Ben Jonson, who was buried upright in Westminster, now being reduced to rubble! The loud sound of an explosion, followed by a terrible echo, as if it were the anguished cry of God; this now brought Westminster Abbey to its knees and melting point, soon everything was gone!

Laundry swiped his phone and ended the call; he and his partner had no words for this terror and so they reverted to the search. Very soon, within this manic hunt, another muffled gunshot was heard.

"Stop! Stop!" Landry shouted as he put his fingers to his lips to produce stillness.

"Shush. Shush! I heard another gun shot." Landry insisted. The team all drew closer and listened intently. Nothing else was heard.

"Landry, look around, the team has all but demolished this building, maybe we are in the wrong place and still catching at straws." Riley indicated.

"I know what I heard and we are missing something in this place." Landry asserted and paced around the room in deep thought. Then he broke his silence.

"The Viet Cong cleverly used underground tunnel networks so I still have a gut feeling that there is something under this place." Landry asserted and continued.

"If we have to go into the sewer to find out, then we will." He heatedly said.

There and then, he hastily turned and pulled out his phone to contact the Environmental Department. He also asked Riley to contact Thames Water. Landry knew that there were large Victorian sewers within this city.

As his fingers punched the phone keys with intense energy, he panted in urgency since solutions had to be found, increasing destruction had to be averted.

Chapter Thirty

After the heat of the fight and firing the shot had dissipated, Lenny nervously dropped the gun. Jay stopped holding Addison's head and rushed over to where Kendal and the man had fallen. Blood was flowing from in between the two bodies and the two men were so closely intertwined, that it was very difficult to see who had been shot. Lenny feared that it was possible that the bullet had hit both men.

Drenched in distraught air and also racked with fear, Lenny's anxiety and all other emotions which were unhinging his mind, propelled him to rapidly pull the two men apart. Jay was overwrought but joined in to help Lenny.

"Kendal! Kendal!" Lenny screamed and Jay also yelled out Kendal's name but no answer came. With this noise, Addison came around and he scrambled to his feet, fell but dragged himself up again and finally reached Jay and Lenny.

He then joined in shifting the two men apart. They rolled Kendal onto his back and could see that his entire chest was soaked with blood. Lenny slapped his face, then he looked at the man, he too was blood splattered but Lenny had no time for him right now as he lay still and lifeless.

"Kendal! Kendal!" Lenny shouted again.

"You killed them both!" Jay sobbed as Addison tried to move her away and then put his ear to Kendal's chest while Lenny held his head.

"His heart is still beating!" Addison cried out.

"Quick. CPR!" Addison shouted and rapidly went to work on Kendal.

After a few minutes he slowly came around and the three watched him with anxious eyes. He was dazed, coughing and gasping for air. They carefully looked him over. He was not shot.

"Thank God! I thought that I had killed you." Lenny exclaimed as he helped Addison raise Kendal's head.

"You alright now, man?" Lenny questioned.

"Very sore, my ribs hurt and I think that he almost killed me. He crushed my air supply. I lost it. Man, I just passed out." Kendal described and went on.

"What happened to him? Where is he?" Kendal nervously asked.

Lenny then flew over to the man. He looked cautiously and could see that he was mortally wounded in the side of his head. Blood was flowing right down to his chest.

"The bastard's dead!" Lenny softly exclaimed.

"We have to stop that machine, interrupt that deadly programme." Kendal speedily said as he struggled to get up. Lenny and Addison pulled him to his feet.

"We should get out of here fast; suppose he has more friends? We will be dead." Jay sobbed once more as she shook her head from side to side.

She then ran over to Sage who was drifting in and out of consciousness and sat just looking at her.

"No time to waste let's look at that machine or else we will all be dead or worse, living under North Korea's rule!" Kendal claimed.

The three young men rushed over to the machine. Lenny stepped to the front and then looked at the back of it.

"Man, this looks like a mass of dials, levers and buttons all designed for mass confusion!" Lenny observed as Kendal looked it over once more.

"This computer controls it, I think." Kendal hesitantly confessed.

"It needs a password to access it." He next informed as he took up his position at the key board.

"You mean, we still in the shit?" Jay remarked from where she was sitting.

Lenny and Addison watched and also tried to think of the impossible task of breaking into this machine.

"What the hell, will we do? Oh God! I think I am beginning to sound just like Jay." Lenny admitted as Kendal tapped one sequence of words after the next.

"Let's try, undercover or fraud, he was posing as that bearded old man so maybe that could be the password." Addison suggested these random key words.

Kendal tried and tried but access was denied each time. The clock was ticking; it was now 17:45. Kendal looked at Lenny and Addison. He really did not know what to do. He tried every sequence of possible words and numbers but they were all incorrect. Then suddenly, Lenny made an outburst.

"What was different and unique about that badass man? Think, think!" Lenny screamed at everybody as he walked directly over to Jay and screamed once more.

"Think. Think!" He yelled.

Kendal stared at Lenny and was getting even more worried now as Lenny kept on repeating the word, think. Maybe all this has broken his mind. Lenny paced the floor with eyes staring and hands on his head. Suddenly, he stood in front of Jay and stared at her and shouted again.

"Mona Lisa! Think! Fucking think!" Lenny screeched.

Jay turned away from Lenny's burning stare and then, she softly whispered.

"Steel. Try S T E E L." She whimpered.

Without delay, Kendal's fingers were about to hit the keyboard but he paused and everyone stared at him from their underwater horror; they were drowning in sweat and despair. Ignoring the stares, Kendal closed his eyes and prayed at this, their darkest hour. Then he tapped in, S T E E L. They held their breath and almost died from the brief wait, and then Kendal jumped up.

"Yes! Yes! We're in!" Kendal bellowed and set to work to disable the programme sequence. They were watching the clocks on the screens and they only had five minutes to free Britain. Addison and Lenny looked over Kendal's shoulder. He pressed keys like a man possessed.

Jay huddled with the semi-conscious Sage and at that moment, like a thunderbolt, a tremendous cacophony, a severe, jarring and jumbled set of sounds could be heard bursting into the room.

"Police! Police! Hands in the air! Don't fucking move!" Landry bellowed at them and continued.

"Down on the ground! Down on the ground! Down on the fucking ground! Now!" He barked louder.

The young people were taken by surprise and now, by another type of abject fear. They froze and did not comply with the bombshell of orders now being levelled at them. Guns were sharply thrust at them.

"I said fucking, down on the ground! On the ground! Get your fucking hands off that computer! Down on the ground!" Landry yelled once more.

While tactical officers rushed forward with weapons directly aiming closer at all of the young people.

With reality quickly sinking in, the four scrambled and went down on the ground. Kendal raised his head to speak but an officer put his foot on his head and pushed him flat. Kendal felt the handcuffs being slapped on to his hands and thick drops of perspiration fell from his body. Next, they were all pulled to standing position.

"Cuff that one over there, seems stoned out of her mind." Riley ordered as he motioned to Sage who had collapsed.

"What do we have here?" Landry asked as he looked each one over.

"You are the ones from that All Wired Up place. And you, Lenny! Are in this with them? You two are wanted for murder." Landry declared looking at Lenny and Kendal.

"Look officer, we have just three minutes-." Kendal was about to explain but was sharply cut off by Riley.

"You giving us ultimatums? Mixed up in what looks like espionage, terrorist acts and murder!" Landry accused as he glared at Kendal.

"Look man this is serious shit and we ain't the guilty ones. That machine there has to be stopped otherwise Britain is history." Lenny explained and went on.

"You know my petty shit but this is really deep shit man!" Lenny pleaded.

"Kendal here, was on that computer trying to stop that death machine." Lenny speedily outlined.

Landry and Riley listened to Lenny but seemed unconvinced. Kendal stepped in with his own plea.

"Let me go back to try to stop that machine or we all die. Just two minutes to hell!" Kendal coldly explained.

Landry and Riley briefly looked at each other but Lenny jumped in yet again.

"You wasting time man, unlock him. I ain't even had children! I can't die yet!" Lenny pleaded.

Landry and Riley looked at Lenny and then at Kendal, and swiftly unlocked the handcuffs.

They watched as Kendal set to work in a frenetic and energetic manner. He hit several keys as though he was exacting punishment on the computer.

After a few alarming moments everyone could hear the low winding down sound of the buzzing. The infernal machine abruptly shut down and all movement died.

"We stopped it!" Kendal declared as Lenny and the others joyfully stared.

"Now we need some fast explaining. It is one minute to 1800 hours and the Prime Minister will need to be updated as a matter of urgency." Landry quickly stated.

Landry, Riley and their team, heard a summary of this elaborate scheme which was almost completely wrought and achieved. As they quickly turned to walk away to use their phones, they heard Lenny's cry once more.

"Uh uh, uh? Aren't you forgetting something?" Lenny hurriedly said as he turned his back to them and shook his handcuffs. Landry nodded his head to an officer who walked over and released Lenny.

"My friends too." Lenny demanded.

Other officers then removed all handcuffs. Landry and Riley next turned away to use their phones but Lenny interjected yet again.

"Skype the Prime Minister from here! This is the scene of the crime of the century, man!" Lenny declared.

"Sorry, but we have to report to the Prime Minister on a secure line." Landry explained as he turned away to use his phone.

The others remained silent and quietly watched but Lenny looked on with a disappointed face and could not help himself for making his case. He quickly cleared his throat and spoke loud and directly to the officers, preventing them from moving away.

"You really mean to tell me that I will miss my chance to be up close and personal with the Prime Minister?" Lenny asked with a broad smile on his face.

Chapter Thirty-One

Eighteen months later, Franz Schubert's Ave Maria, written in 1826, streamed through the June air of the Church,https://www.youtube.com/watch?v=5NARW5X5zh8&list=RD5NARW5X5zh8&start_radio=1. (listen here).

Everyone present, listened with admiration and love. Schubert called his piece 'Ellens *dritter Gesang'*, Ellen's third song, and it was written as a prayer to the Virgin Mary from a frightened girl, Ellen Douglas, who had been forced into hiding. (Song Facts.com)

This beautiful melodious piece, piped into the hearts and minds of everyone present at the wedding of Kendal and Sage. The loving couple stood at the altar waiting ready to pledge and seal their love, for now and always. Their hearts were overflowing and the children stood behind them with bright smiles and happy anticipation of a new and stable family life.

Lenny and Addison stood beside Kendal, probably as the first pair, to be designated as best men at a wedding. Three months earlier, Kendal had reciprocated for Addison, in his marriage to Jay.

The city of London was recovering and slowly getting back to normal. The attacks had all been passed off as being orchestrated by a 'lone wolf, Jian Ling.' It was reported that he had been caught and killed as he was hiding out in London's China Town, in a restaurant which had been burnt to the ground, the Dragon Tooth. It was also reported, that Parker Davies and his accomplice Mae Young, had been killed while committing a robbery at the All Wired Up Company, where Sage had been working. Unfortunately, Sage was taken hostage by Jian Ling as his conspiracy unfolded.

The five young people and their relatives had been taken to a countryside facility for counselling and therapy. When they were released, amazingly enough, they had no recollection of being involved in any National Security activities. Sage's alleged murder, Kendal and Lenny's arrest, were reported, as all a case of mistaken identity, no 'scheme was ever mentioned.

Other Books by This Author
Alexis V

Engulfing Events is a series of three crime fiction novels, written by Alexis V. The series has a multi-cultural setting within South America and the Caribbean, and follows the young characters, Erica Durr, Ethan Miller, Sofia Grant and Carlos Carrillo as they battle through a mine field of unsolicited trouble and dangerous life shaking encounters.

The novels in this trilogy are titled, Girl Arrested release date 2015, Child Taken, 2016 and Fear Undetermined, release date 2018. Each novel although part of a series, is its own standalone story, with a complete climax within the book. You don't need to read the next novel to get to the ending but if you do, you are guaranteed not to be disappointed.

Books

A troubled and unhappy home life leads young Erica into a secret relationship with an older man. She meets with her lover but later wakes to find herself covered in blood on board her father's yacht and the prime suspect in a murder scene. Luckily she has two allies in the form of best friend Sophia and new neighbour Ethan who over the course of the next few days move heaven and earth to help her clear her name. As they investigate they become immersed in the dark and dangerous world of the illegal gold trade and people trafficking.

Warm tropical waters, idyllic shores, a paradise in the distance; a Caribbean cruise never to be forgotten. Lurking amidst the calm seas is an evil force; unleashing the never ending nightmare when a child is taken! With forty-eight hours to find her, the gates of agony are thrown wide open. The parents and their friends go through hell on earth to save her! They must fight their way past labyrinths and a host of deadly enemies if they are to rescue the child and hold together the family's enduring love and trust.

A wonderful night goes all wrong and lives are thrown into peril when a young pilot is feared to be either violently killed or abducted from his bachelor night pre-wedding party. His name is smeared by being subsequently accused of attempting to kill his rich father and suspected of staging his own disappearance. His fiancée and two best friends must find out what happened to him before it is too late. There is one problem, the trail leads them to one of the most dangerous and deadly places on earth, the Amazon.

Love In The Shadows

ALEXIS V

Rebekah Fuller's main encouragement through her limiting teenage years was her friendship with Annabelle Foster, a pretty and popular girl. The two girls meet the boys of each other's dreams but still managed to fall deeply in love, at a time when war is declared and lives are hurled into uncertainty and confusion! The war and Rebekah's mother's excessive tendency to overprotect, sweeps her into a minefield of uncharted pitfalls and dramatic life changes. These dynamics, not only determine Rebekah's future but her passions, her pains, her hopes and dreams. They lead her to several emotional valleys but would she manage to finally reach love's mountain top?

Life In The Tickbox
ALEXIS V.

How do you imagine your future? Imagining the future helps us to prepare for problems and be more equipped to solve them but what if your entire future was totally and absolutely within the hands of the State? A State which was based on scoring and your ability for happiness, success and health, rested in those ratings. What would you do? Would you contemplate to leave or to remain? This mini-story is a funny view of things which may possibly come to pass; with hidden truths but powerful meanings!

The Last Time

Alexis V

For many, counterfeit love can masquerade as genuine affection, through manipulation and control. Occurring often during young years, from not wanting to be left out from life's constants and reinforced by great sex. All these fuel a bad bond leading to relationship entrapment. Options for getting out and starting over, appear elusive and emotional walls crumble. Life becomes buried beneath regret and the cycle of hopelessness spins. This short story is a glimpse of the life of a young woman which exposes these relationship issues. Can she find the strength to get out?

Enduring Memories Of Someone Special
By Alexis V.

A splendid inspirational keepsake, which is an ideal gift for family and friends of any special, loved one. It's filled with heartwarming sentiments, a page with blank lines to insert a personalized recipient's and sender's details. Suitable for a daughter, sister, mother, friend or any woman who has touched the lives of others and has 'passed on' but whose life remains as 'Enduring Memories.'

An Inspirational keepsake of a collection of comforting thoughts, that can be given to the family and friends of a special loved one. An excellent memento for any person who has touched the lives of others and has 'passed on' but whose life remains as a 'Special Memory.' Includes, a blank page which can be personalized and one for written reflections.

Find Your Mountain

Alexis V.

One young woman's view of her struggle to reveal her true 'identity' to her Caribbean heritage parents and extended family. She clearly understood the torment which ensued for many people to reconcile and understand that she was an individual, unique and with specific differences. She knew that there would be an outpouring of support for her if perhaps she had a terminal illness but there were explicit and understood principles governing and surrounding her 'difference' and often within the Caribbean there was little mercy.

Who gets to be happy? This short comic narrative is a satire which exposes the result of experiences of living in a world of rising tensions and negative emotions; where the relentless focus on skin colour precludes acceptance of this twin and severely limits their life chances. This brother and sister set out to exact revenge on those they judged to be guilty of restricting their self-worth but can they execute the deadly deeds?

House

Alexis V.

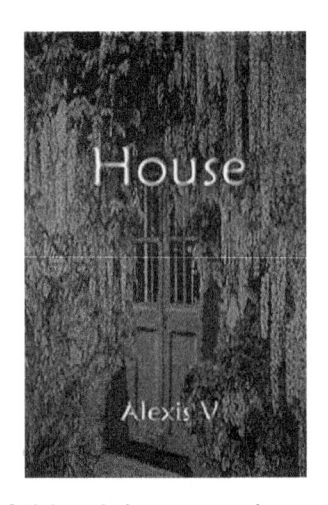

At the start of this nightmare, she was unable to see how to get out of what she thought was clearly a very sinister dream. She was holding her frozen brain within her head; it offered no course of action for her shaky limbs to take. She was wide awake and walking so this eerie place was indeed not any dream. This was supposed to have been a mere simple viewing of an empty property. But laying bare before her eyes from surreal shows, she was made to think that, 'if our choices in life make us who we are, then who are we?' If you dare read this dark undefinable tale of chilling life echoes which rebound from the wounded place where they were born.

`Concept Children's Books

Is your child a 'runner,' or perhaps one who is autistic with Special Education Needs? Then this book can provide support for helping the child who frequently runs off to understand when it is safe to run and when it is dangerous to do so. The young child and in particular the autistic child, often does not have real awareness of dangers in their environment. This book can provide support to your child in developing safety awareness.

Gordon Reads about **Making Choices**

In adolescent years, teenagers can make judgments and decisions on their own but most often in situations where they have time to think. On the other hand, when they have to make quick decisions or in social situations, their choices are often influenced by external elements like the peer group. Read to find out about the different types of choices teenagers face. See if Gordon can resist pressure from others and as a teenager, can you?

Understanding, colour, shape and size are essentials which children need to know in order to master Reading, Writing, Language and Mathematics. It is a tool for learning many skills in all subject areas. For autistic children who are mostly visual thinkers and learners, color, shape and size can be used to create learning steps, helping them to pick up words and concepts, and develop basic skills. Ultimately, the goal is to motivate the child to develop better verbal communication skills. Thomas Reads about Colour, Shape and size, can be used to stimulate awareness of these concepts.

Emily Reads about Making Friends

Written by Alexis V
Illustrated by Peter Vincent

Building friendships can be challenging for any child and especially so for the SEN child who may require additional support as a result of a broad range of needs. These needs may be in regard to emotional and behavioural difficulties, or how the child relates to and behaves with other people. This book is intended to deliberately focus on key social skills to support the child in developing friendships.

Thank you for sharing in my imagination.

Alexis V